Peacocks

A Licking Thicket Novella

Lucy Lennox

May Archer

Peacocks

Lane's Tips for Licking Thicket Newcomers

If at all possible, find yourself a hot and helpful landlord like Jaybird Proud who mows the lawn shirtless... and hope your grass grows quickly.

Expect the unexpected at work. If you're a veterinarian, this might mean letter-cows, pet pigs that aren't pets, and Butterscotch the Pomeranian, who has Strong Feelings about his glands.

Offer your help around town when needed... especially when that gorgeous landlord knocks on your door because his (pea)cock won't stop displaying.

Learn about local customs, including: matchmaking, leaving Italian Gentlemen on the doormat, ordering tater tots, and entwining dead vines into wreaths as a sign of true love.

Get your car washed on the regular... especially when your landlord is the one doing the scrubbing.

Above all, keep things casual, even when Jay ends up at your place every night. And every morning. And the occasional afternoon.

But when you find yourself falling for someone like Jaybird Proud (and life in his weird and wonderful town), let go of everything you thought you wanted... and Entwine that Thicketeer forever.

Chapter One

Lane

AFTER MY LAST disaster of a relationship, in which I'd been accused of being "a master of emotional evasion" who was "fundamentally indifferent toward romantic partnerships"—don't date a law professor, people, just *don't*—I never expected to find myself interested in another man.

And even if I had? Even if, somewhere in a sealed-shut compartment in the back of my brain, there existed a part of me that wasn't *entirely* "indifferent toward romantic partnerships" on the whole?

I'd sure as hell never expected the object of my fascination could be someone like Jaybird Proud.

Jaybird had offered to rent me the apartment over his garage when I moved to Licking Thicket six months ago... then refused to cash my rent checks because I was his cousin Charlie's boyfriend's friend, which "practically makes us family, Lane!"—an assessment I disagreed with on many, many levels.

Jaybird greeted me most evenings, come rain or come shine, with a bright, handsome smile, a cheery "Howdy, neighbor!" and occasionally the offer of a dinner casserole.

Or a beer. Or, on one memorable occasion, a "dirt cake"... whatever the hell that was.

Jaybird wore snap-back hats with misspelled John *Dear* logos ("on account of Kitten Montgomery's confusion at Valentine's Day while working the embroidery machine," Jaybird had explained. "But I don't wanna make her feel bad by not wearing it, do I?").

Jaybird's career ambition began and ended with working at the Suds Barn as a full-time Automobile Cleansing Artisan (not joking) because "there's nothin' more satisfying than settin' things to rights."

Jaybird had never met a T-shirt with sleeves that hadn't seen the sharp edge of a pair of scissors (which, okay... shoutout to Jesus for that one) even when the weather turned cold.

He was like a splinter under my skin. Too silly to take seriously, too friendly to be genuine, and too sexy not to fantasize about... sometimes multiple times a night.

"The man's gonna drive me to drink," I admitted to my friend Hunter before taking a bite of my ham and swiss. I only had a half-hour lunch break today between a morning full of spay and neuter surgeries and an afternoon packed with wellness appointments, so I was glad Hunter had agreed to get to the Thicket Tavern early and order for us.

Hunter had heard my complaints often enough now that he didn't bother asking for clarification.

"What's Jaybird done now?" He crunched a cucumber slice, looking way too amused at my plight.

"Cleaned the ice off my windshield this morning," I muttered. "Mirrors too. Said he didn't want my fingers to freeze off before I did surgery this morning. Who does that?"

Hunter let out a low whistle. "Diabolical."

"It *is*," I insisted.

I knew I probably sounded ridiculous, but I simply didn't understand *why* Jaybird did the things he did. In my experience, people didn't do nice things—not so many nice things, at least, and not all in a row—for no reason.

But try as I might, I couldn't puzzle out what Jaybird's agenda was.

If he was a dog, or a cat, or even a turkey, like Hunter and Charlie's pet, Tammy Wynette, I'd have known exactly what he wanted and how to handle him.

Men had always been much, much harder for me to read... and unfortunately for me, Jaybird was undeniably a man.

All six feet and several sexy inches of him.

"You know... you could move out," Hunter suggested. "Morris and Danica Borris are retiring down to Georgia and selling their spread."

I glanced up at him. "Morris *Borris*?"

He ignored me. "You'd like their place. Ten acres at the edge of town. Super quiet. River access for fly fishing. It's exactly what you talked about when you considered moving up here."

My stomach twisted at the idea.

Yes, fishing had been one of the draws of moving to Licking Thicket from Athens last summer. There had been many. First and foremost was the opportunity to escape the quasi-scandal that had resulted from my breakup with Professor Chadwick Montgomery. The University of Georgia was a big school but a tiny town, and if I'd had to respond to one more well-meaning, whisper-voiced, "How you doing with, uh... with Chad's wedding and all?" I was going to lose it.

Second, my teaching job had gotten stale. It had begun

feeling too far away from the actual practice of veterinary medicine, and I came to realize I hadn't held a live animal in months.

And third, I'd wanted a place of my own. Animals of my own.

And—in whatever form I could find it—peace.

The small town of Licking Thicket in Tennessee had not been in my top twenty "towns to move to" list, but then Hunter had contacted me to tell me about the opportunity to buy into a thriving vet practice in his hometown. Fate seemed to have decided for me, and now that I was here, I had to admit I was happy with my decision. The town was much more gay-friendly than I'd imagined, and the vet practice was even better than I'd expected.

The doctor I'd partnered with was funny as shit too. Alva's dry humor kept my workdays moving quickly, and her desire to move over to the large animal part of the practice meant I could take charge of everything else.

That part of the move was going well. It was the social part that was lagging.

"I'm not sure I'm ready to move," I hedged. "Work's been nonstop, and Jay's place is awfully convenient to the clinic."

Hunter glanced up at me with a forkful of salad halfway to his mouth. "Jaybird lives on the opposite side of town. The Borris place is half the distance from the clinic."

I let out a grunt before taking another bite of my sandwich. Hunter studied me while he chewed. "What else is Jay doing that's getting on your nerves? Couple months back, it was the... lawn mowing? You said he wasn't doing it right?"

The memory of that day still got under my skin. "He mows in a giant circle! Normal people do it in straight lines.

Back and forth. Hell, do it at an angle if you want to get fancy. But this guy? He does it in a spiral that's enough to make you get seasick from watching."

Hunter gave me a sly look. "And you were... watching?"

I opened my mouth to snap back, *Of course I was watching. Have you seen the man?* But I clamped my teeth closed before the words could escape. Hunter didn't need to know I had an embarrassingly strong physical attraction to my landlord.

"It was hard to miss him when he was wearing nothing but tiny cutoff shorts and work boots," I muttered, admitting my fetish reluctantly. "Besides, he's accident-prone, and one of these days, it's bound to involve arterial spray. I'm just looking out for myself, considering he's still not charging me rent."

"Jaybird Proud? Accident-prone? The man is the first to volunteer for tree removal after bad thunderstorms. He has, like, three kinds of chainsaws. He does engine maintenance and rides dirt bikes. Hell, the man whittles, for fuck's sake. You can trust him around a mower blade."

An older man I didn't recognize leaned over from the table next to ours. "And Jay twines a mean vine, if you know what I mean."

I... did not know what he meant. "I'm sorry?" I asked politely.

The woman with him, a lady I recognized as owning a poodle-rottweiler mix, nodded. "He's talking about the Entwinin'. You probably don't know about it yet, being brand-new to town and all, Dr. Lane. The Entwinin' is sort of like the Thicket version of Valentine's Day."

"'Cept it happens in April," the man said, like this made any sense whatsoever. "And there ain't no candy hearts. Only good, solid wood."

The woman patted his hand. "He means wisteria vines. It's town tradition to weave the vines into a symbol of love and gift it to your sweetheart."

"What does that have to do with Jaybird?" I asked.

"Oh, Jay." The woman got a dreamy look on her face. "Folks around here call him the Entwinin' Whisperer. He does the most beautiful wreaths and items for the holiday. In fact, just last year, he twined a birdhouse in the shape of a tractor for Misty Willard. You might spot it if you head down the Nuthatch Road."

Small towns were strange. I already knew this. Athens, Georgia, had a law against offering two-for-one drinks. You could offer half-priced drinks, but not two for the price of one. They also had a tree that owned its own land, a haunted sorority house, and a building with a tree for a roof.

But at no time did someone craft a tractor birdhouse out of wisteria.

At least now, I supposed I knew what he was doing in his garage workroom all those nights when I came home.

"How... nice," I said when what I really meant was, "*May I please finish my sandwich in peace?*"

Ava Siegel walked by with a baby strapped to her chest. I'd learned from her visits to the clinic with her one-eyed cat that Ava always had a child of some kind on her person. It didn't even need to be hers. In fact, I was fairly sure this one was related to the family that owned a beautiful pair of two-eyed Siamese cats. "Jay also carves tots... and toys."

I glanced at Hunter and murmured, "Does she mean Toys for Tots?"

He shook his head and grinned. "You'd think so, but no. And before you ask, you do not have time for this story. Suffice it to say that, around here, tater tots aren't just potatoes. I'll explain it all to you later."

I focused on finishing my sandwich while the rest of them spoke around me about Jay's "eye for design" and his "willingness to chip in" around town.

That part I already knew. Jay seemed to be everywhere, all the time, no matter where I went. It was awful. And wonderful.

If I needed my car washed, he'd be working at the Suds Barn, crooning at the car about how it was a noble beast and deserved to be clean, *yes it did, yes it did.*

If I needed groceries, he was in line ahead of me, joking with the cashier about the Licking Thicket Bovines' chances of making it to the state championships this year.

If I needed my car washed again, he'd be at the Suds Barn once more, wearing a superhero costume for a full month before Halloween and calling himself Captain Clean.

If I stopped at Chuy's Barbershop to get a trim, he was there dropping off a bundle of firewood and discussing the merits of pellet stoves versus hardwood for reliable whole-home heating.

If I needed my car washed yet again, he'd *still* be at the Suds Barn, singing a falsetto rendition of "Car Wash" while punctuating every word with a sway of his hips when he got to the "*workin' at the car wash, yeahhh*" part of the chorus.

If I went to the library, I might find him reorganizing the gardening section and chatting with patrons while Chad the librarian looked on with a smile... though he'd have violently *shushed* anyone else.

And if I needed my car washed... well, you get the picture.

And *yes*, I suppose I did make a lot of trips to the car wash. The man had a killer body, and it happened to look amazing in damp denim and threadbare cotton tees, okay?

And I couldn't help it if living in the countryside was *dusty*.

I sighed and stood up, crumpling my sandwich paper and taking a final sip of my drink. "Thanks for meeting me. Sorry it was so short."

Hunter stood up and gathered his own trash. "Want me to send you the info on the Borris place, or are you going to freeload off Jaybird a little while longer?"

I hadn't thought of it as freeloading. I'd been more than willing to pay Jay rent, and he'd refused, so I figured he was okay with me staying there.

I frowned. "You think he wants me out so he can rent the place to someone else?"

Hunter shrugged. "Who knows? Man seems to be a sucker for a pretty face. First Charlie, now you. Wonder if he'd finally start charging if a plain-looking lady moved in."

I stared at him. "You're acting like Jay is *gay*," I said, whispering the last word like an old lady gossiping about someone's angina.

Hunter's eyebrows dipped in confusion. "Uh... that's 'cause he is?"

I stood up straighter and inhaled a breath for patience. "Hunter. The man knows how to string a bow and fletch an arrow."

He nodded. "Okay?"

"He knows at least seventy-five percent of the starting roster of the Tennessee football team."

"Sure. Big Vols fan," he agreed. It was Hunter's turn to frown. "Are you saying gay men don't follow sports? Because that's weird and also wildly inaccurate."

I narrowed my eyes at him. "Name one wide receiver in the NFL, current or retired."

Hunter opened his mouth to respond but hesitated

when he realized I had him. "This isn't about me," he said with a sniff. "Besides, you don't know any either."

"That is *exactly* my point," I hissed.

"Peerless Price," someone muttered nearby. "Saw him once when he played with the Falcons."

I didn't even justify the interference with a glance. I'd been in the Thicket long enough to have learned to ignore the nosy nellies. They were like forest fires. If you gave them more fuel, it only made the flames last longer.

I moved away from the crowded tables and tossed my garbage in the can before turning to Hunter and lowering my voice even more. "Jay can't be gay. He's having an affair with Blythe Nelson! She's over twice a week like clockwork and stays until well past midnight."

Not that I paid much attention. Obviously.

Jaybird Proud's love life was none of my business.

I just happened to share a driveway with the man and couldn't help it if his girlfriend's obnoxious minivan took up half my view every Wednesday and Friday night.

Hunter threw back his head and laughed. "Now I'm a little worried about your mental acuity, my friend. First of all, Blythe is happily married to the world's quirkiest ophthalmologist. Secondly, she's pregnant with her third child."

"Don't you think I know that? It's disgusting. Both of them should be ashamed of themselves. Unless... well, unless she's in an open relationship, I guess."

"Definitely not," he said with a laugh. "But she is head over heels for her husband and has asked Jay to teach her how to make a giant Entwinin' wreath in the shape of a bunch of pairs of eyeglasses for her husband's practice to display this April."

Oh. But that meant... I closed my eyes and groaned. "That... would make more sense than the other thing."

"You think? Lane. Bro. *Buddy.* I'm a little worried about you. Do you think maybe you've been working too many hours at the clinic? You seem to have taken jumping-to-conclusions lessons from the worst of the Thicket gossips. Is it Alva? Is she a bad influence?"

I thought about my business partner and her respect for the townsfolk's privacy. "It's not Alva."

Hunter tilted his head before grinning at me. "Then maybe it's jealousy."

"Jealousy?" I squawked. "Me? *Me?* I don't get jealous. Just ask Chad."

I screwed up my face, remembering some of my ex's parting comments about me not caring about anything that didn't "have fur or feathers" and his desire to find a man who "actually paid attention to him."

Even a year later, the words stung... maybe in part because they were true.

"Besides," I went on seriously, "Blythe Nelson isn't my type! Jesus, Hunter."

He barked out a laugh as we walked into the chill of the afternoon. "Lane, let me put this in a way you might under-stand. You know how turkeys sometimes strut and puff out their chest and drag their wings on the ground?"

I gave him a worried look. "Hunter, your Tammy is a hen, not a tom. She shouldn't be strutting—"

He huffed. "She's not. I meant... look, you know how cows wiggle their tails? Or how wolves will bring a kill back to their den to share it? Or how penguins give each other pebbles?" He leaned closer and wiggled his eyebrows. "Or how stags sometimes butt their antlers into trees because they really want to be butting other things into... other places?"

I stared at him slack-jawed. "Wait... really?"

Hunter nodded with satisfaction. "Now you're getting it."

"Hunter." I put a hand on his arm. "If Tammy is exhibiting *any* of those behaviors, please bring her to the clinic. It could be serious."

He laughed. "Okay, you're *not* getting it. I'm not talking about my turkey, Lane. I'm talking about you and your landlord."

I shook my head. I felt stupid for not getting his point, but I really couldn't see what stag ruts and wolf kills had to do with Jaybird's constant presence in my space.

Hunter put a hand on my arm. "Maybe you should ask your landlord who he's really got his eye on," he explained. "You might be surprised by his response."

Hold up. Did Hunter mean he thought Jay was interested in...? With... *me?*

No. Not possible.

Jay was friendly, yes. Neighborly. Strangely, even *aggressively*, thoughtful. But he was like that with everyone, it seemed.

And even if, through some fluke of nature, he *was* interested in me... the two of us had about as much in common as a... a cow and a rabbit. A rainbow trout and a mourning dove. I liked looking at him, sure, but he wasn't meant for me.

I was too embarrassed—and late to work—to stick around and interrogate Hunter further. Instead, I bolted back to the clinic and busied myself with vaccinations and well checks. When I finally left, it was almost eight o'clock.

It was pitch-dark, and the cold air immediately sank into my bones.

The sandwich was long gone, and my stomach rumbled with the need for dinner. There were several enticing options awaiting me upstairs at my place. I could scramble some eggs, pour a bowl of cornflakes, or even microwave a chicken tikka if I was feeling fancy.

My eyes betrayed me as I pulled into the driveway by straying immediately to Jay's parking spot. His truck was there, and warm lamplight glowed in the windows of the house.

He was home, but tonight, he wasn't outside to greet me. The garage where he was often working was closed, for once.

My breath hitched, imagining him inside, dancing to the country music he liked to play. One time, I'd caught him grilling out in the yard, singing into his spatula while his steak sizzled. Another time, I'd seen him through the window, singing into a can of cooking spray while he baked something that smelled cinnamony.

He was silly and playful, and there was something about his freedom to be his unique self that...

Okay, fine. That attracted me to him.

Maybe we were less like a trout and a dove and more like a yappy Jack Russell terrier and a derpy golden retriever.

My eyes remained riveted to his kitchen window as I stepped out of my own vehicle and closed the door. There was no sign of him inside. I finally gave up and focused on making it up the stairs to my apartment without face-planting on the remnants of this morning's ice... when I noticed something on the Welcome mat in front of my apartment door.

It was a glass Tupperware dish with a blue plastic lid. My heart thumped erratically.

I leaned down to pick it up and immediately inhaled the perfect blend of garlic and tomato sauce that indicated something wonderfully Italian inside.

It wasn't the first time Jay had left dinner for me. Not even the tenth. In fact, my first week in the Thicket had been so chaotic and unpredictable that Jay had left dinner for me every single night.

I caught myself grinning as I cradled the warm casserole dish against my chest like a lovesick teenager holding a bouquet of flowers and entered the apartment. As soon as I set it down on the kitchen table and peeled off the lid, I saw it was one of my favorites.

A huff of laughter escaped me as I remembered the first time I'd thanked him for this dish.

"Of all the things you've ever made, this one might be my favorite," I'd admitted. "You have no idea how grateful I was to come home to a warm meal last night. Mrs. Estrada's pug had nine puppies, and none of them came easy. Thank you so much."

He'd beamed at me. "I call it Italian Gentleman," he'd said proudly, nodding down at the dish. "On account of the bow tie pasta."

I dished a heap of bow ties into a bowl and threw it in the microwave for a few seconds while moving over to my dresser to change out of my work clothes. I'd just slipped on a soft pair of cotton lounge pants and was getting ready to search for a clean T-shirt when there was a knock on my door.

I glanced over to see Jay standing on the other side of the glass-paned door, staring at me. His arms were bare, as usual, but he'd thrown a vest over his sleeveless shirt in deference to the cold.

Our eyes met, skyrocketing my heart rate and making my skin tingle.

Was he truly gay? Was he truly interested in me? And what would I do if he was?

Jaybird Proud was my exact opposite.

He was the kind of guy who flew by the seat of his pants while I meticulously planned out everything in my life.

He was a chaotic collection of mismatched tools and scraps of lumber while I prided myself on perfectly arranged and sanitized surgical instruments and supplies organized to within an inch of their lives.

I had advanced veterinary degrees and teaching accreditations... while Jay probably claimed the School of Hard Knocks on his social media profile.

I liked reading and period dramas; he enjoyed chainsaws and... apparently creating things out of dead wisteria.

My eyes trailed down his muscular body while I moved to answer the door, yanking the T-shirt over my head quickly to keep him from seeing my hardening nipples... among other things.

I needed to stop thinking these things. To get Hunter's earlier words out of my brain and get things back to normal with my landlord... for whatever definition of *normal* applied to our relationship.

But as soon as I opened the door, I noticed he was wringing his hands worriedly, and the other thoughts fled my brain.

"Jay?" I asked in concern. "Is everything okay?"

"No. I mean, yes. I mean... I don't know." He glanced everywhere but at me, looking nervous for the first time in the six months I'd known him.

"What's going on?"

"I need your help. I, uh..." He finally met my eyes and firmed his jaw defiantly. "I need help with my cock."

15

Chapter Two

Jay

It wasn't easy asking people for help.

It *especially* wasn't easy when the person I needed help from was Dr. Lane Desmond. He was beautiful, successful, smart... basically everything I wasn't. That was why I'd waited so long to throw myself on his mercy.

But this wasn't just about me and my hopeless crush on my tenant. There were innocent animals involved. And the smitten pet owners of the Thicket didn't just sigh dreamily about how good-looking Lane was; they said he really knew his animals too.

Then again, though, maybe he didn't since he was looking at me like I had three heads.

"I'm sorry?" he asked. "Could you repeat that?"

"Look, I know you just got home, and you've had a real busy day. I hate to bother you." I swallowed hard and tried not to stare at Lane, which was a tricky thing since the chilly air had his nipples poking against the soft cotton of his T-shirt, and a burst of his distinct Lane scent—a heady combo of cologne, laundry detergent, and lemon disinfectant that somebody really needed to bottle up in one of those air-freshener plugs because *holy shit* was it sexy— came wafting out the door at me.

"The thing is…" I spread my hands helplessly. "I've done all I know how to do, but he won't tuck his feathers."

"Your… It won't… *Tuck its feathers?*" he repeated, aghast.

"I dunno what the technical term is." I shrugged. "Deflate? Settle? Move from red alert down to a nice, peaceable yellow?"

"And we're talking about your…" He paused expectantly, and if I didn't know better—if I didn't know for sure that Lane was one hundred percent immune to my charms, such as they were—I'd almost have thought he snuck a glance at my groin.

"My… peacock," I repeated slowly. The poor man was tired, and it showed. "Like I said."

Lane squeezed his eyes shut for a second. "You definitely did not say that," he muttered. "Dear God."

"Huh?"

"Nothing." He waved a hand. "Come in, come in." He turned and walked toward the kitchenette.

As I followed him inside, my eyes immediately went to his ass since it would've been wrong not to appreciate the rounded muscles there, and I was the kind of guy who tried to do *right*.

In fact, I was so committed to rightness there wasn't a single time in the past six meonths I hadn't taken the opportunity to stare at Dr. Desmond's significant assets.

While I might not be educated or gifted, I sure as shit wasn't stupid.

"Did you get the food I left?" I asked, suddenly feeling

nervous. "I didn't know... I mean, you might not be hungry. If you don't want it or need it, you can just... throw it out. I mean, maybe don't throw out the Tupperware. That's one of my good ones. But you can..." I spotted the container on the table. "You know what? I'll throw it out for you. It's no trouble—"

I reached for the Tupperware only to be stopped when Lane grabbed my wrist. "Jay, I want it. I'm starving. Please don't throw it out. Italian Gentleman's my favorite."

His kind smile and the feel of his warm grip on my wrist made my stomach tighten. "Oh. Okay." I swallowed again 'cause it was either that or drool. "Good, then."

Lane nodded and let go, moving to the microwave and pulling out a bowl of the pasta. Seeing him eat the food I'd made gave me a feeling of... I didn't know, exactly. Pride? Happiness? I wanted to take care of him, make sure he had what he needed and didn't subsist on peanut butter crackers or cereal like I knew he did sometimes on heavy workdays. I wanted to lighten his load and bring a smile to his face.

He stabbed a fork into the bowl and shoved a giant mouthful of bow ties between his lips. I was mesmerized.

"So... you have a peacock?" he asked in between bites. "What's wrong with him, exactly?"

This didn't seem the right time to explain I had *multiple* peacocks, so I focused on the one for now. "Dave's got a feather issue, like I was explaining."

Lane blinked at me, and when his lips twitched in a smile, I wanted to beat my chest. "Your peacock is named Dave."

"Yep. D-Disco Dave," I agreed, still staring at his lips. "I can't take credit for his name, though. His former owner named him." It didn't seem the right time to explain that either, so I hurried on. "He won't stop... *flaunting*."

Lane stopped with a forkful of pasta halfway to his mouth. "Flaunting?"

I shrugged. "The plumage thing..." I fanned out all ten of my fingers at once in a replica of a peacock's tail. I had a second to be self-conscious—my fingers were blunt and callused from years of hard work, not at all like Lane's fine hands—but the way Lane bit his lip at the sight made my pants tighten.

"When peacocks spread their tail feathers, or *trains*, it's called displaying or... or train rattling," he said, eyes firmly on his pasta. "It's a, uh... a mating thing."

"Right. I knew that much. I also know it's not the season for it. But *Dave* doesn't seem to realize that. And I don't have any peahens, so what's he even doing? I'm worried something's wrong with him. I'm worried it's a little like one of those medicine commercials, you know? Like, if his *displaying* lasts more than four hours, he should see a doctor?"

Lane stuffed the pasta in his mouth to keep from laughing, I could tell, and that made me feel a bit better. Lane wouldn't be laughing if he thought Dave's condition was an emergency.

"How was work today?" I asked, deciding to change the subject. "I heard Sami Nishawn's Doberman was in for a neuter. It's about time. That asshole won't leave Mr. Holcombe's cockapoo alone."

Why did I suddenly feel like I was using the word *cock* too frequently for polite company?

"He came through with flying colors," Lane said after swallowing and reaching for his water glass. "It should calm him down. But I think Mr. Holcombe's cockapoo is the instigator in that situation. Poor thing's bored to tears since

Mr. Holcombe's knee replacement. He hasn't been able to walk her nearly as often."

"I've been walking her every day," I admitted. "She likes going to the little creek at the end of Newell Road. Makes her muddy as fuck, but Mr. Holcombe has a hose right by the back door with hot water to it and everything."

I didn't add that I'd been the one to plumb the hot water to it after Mr. Holcombe had complained about how hard it was to wash off muddy paws in winter. But now that there was a warm water supply, Binnie was living a life of luxury.

Lane studied me while he ate his dinner. "That's awfully generous of you, Jay."

Heat flooded my cheeks. I decided to walk over to the window and look out in hopes they'd cool before Lane noticed. "Nah. Not a big thing. I have time and two good knees, right? Hey, your car running smooth?"

"Mmhm."

"Good. *Good.*" I glanced down at the driveway, squinting to see if there was any sign of his tires being underinflated. "If your tire pressure gauge lights up, let me know, and I'll add more air. Sometimes when it gets this cold, that light comes on and makes you think you're fixing to get a flat. It's just the temperature, though. Tires need a little extra in the winter."

I felt his eyes on me as he ate. Being in his apartment, surrounded by the fancy scents of his home and signs of his private life, made me nervous and excited.

He kept the place neat as a pin. No clutter anywhere. There was a framed photograph on the wall that looked like something out of a modern art museum. Colorful graffiti bathed the underside of a city bridge, the modern spray paint contrasting with the historic metalwork of the struts.

Surrounding the photo were several framed diplomas—fancy college degrees I didn't have and never would.

There was also a pair of novels on a side table with thriller-type titles. On the bottom of the stack was a book on mutual fund investing and one on customer service. My eyes were hungry for more information about him. It seemed everywhere I looked gave me just enough to want more.

But also enough to know a man like him would never be into a guy like me.

I thought about what he might see if he went next door to my place.

Cozy crocheted afghans in an eye-watering variety of colors covered every bed and chair, giving the place an off-kilter, mismatched look... but they'd been gifts from my grandma and her friends for running their errands and fixing their faucets, and love was hooked into every stitch, so I couldn't pack them away, could I?

Pictures of my family papered the walls... but I had a huge clan, and they all came by my place regularly. I'd hate to have someone feel they weren't represented.

I had bunches of financial papers strewn over my desk because owning the Suds Barn wasn't all about the dancing and the cleaning—it required a *lot* of paperwork—and because someone in the Thicket always needed something, and since I had a little bit of money put aside, I liked to help where I could.

And my garage... well, best not to think about what all Jay might find down in the garage. At least none of the noise seemed to be making its way up here... yet.

I swallowed and pointed to the customer service book on the nightstand. "You probably don't need that. Everyone in town says you're doing great and you really know your stuff. I don't have any animals, or I'd be able to say for myself too." I paused, considering. "Well, I guess I do have some now, don't I? With the peacocks and all."

"Peacocks, as in, more than one?" I could hear the amusement in his voice.

"Yeah. It's a long story."

"Long enough to let me finish this food?"

I glanced at him over my shoulder and sighed. It wasn't that there was anything particularly embarrassing about the story, really. But it seemed like the kind of silly thing Lane Desmond would never get himself involved in.

Yet another thing we didn't have in common.

"D'you have any idea how many people want peacocks at their wedding and in their kids' portraits?" I began.

Lane's eyes danced. "You starting a rental peacock enterprise?"

"Not starting one, exactly. More like acquiring one. See, I have this friend..."

"All your stories start like that, Jay," he said. If I wasn't hallucinating, it seemed like there was affection in Lane's voice. "And before you start telling me about it, you need to know that if I'm doing well in customer service here, it's because of you, not me."

I turned to look at him in confusion. "How d'you mean?"

"I told you a couple of months ago I was having a rough time of it, and you went out of your way to introduce me around. Sang my praises and dropped the right words in several people's ears. Don't tell me you didn't because I heard all about it from Alva."

I flapped my hand at him. "Hush. Nothing anyone else wouldn't have done."

"Not true at all," Lane argued. "Plenty of people would-n't've taken the time to do it." He shoveled the last bite of pasta in his mouth and tilted his head to watch me thought-fully as he chewed. "But you did. And I appreciate it."

The weight of his gaze made me squirm in good ways and bad. "It feels nice to help when you can, that's all. Anyway... back to the peacocks." I took a breath to continue my story.

"Actually..." Lane took his empty bowl to the sink and tidied the leftovers into the fridge. "Let's go check on this peacock of yours while you tell me how you came to be in possession of it. *Them.*"

I waited while he grabbed a hoodie. To be fair, I tried not watching his chest and abs while he pulled it on, but once again, it would've been wrong not to appreciate the glory of it up close and personal, in a way I rarely got to. I was only human, after all.

As he slid his feet into his shoes, I cleared my throat. "So, a couple years back, my friend John over in Nuthatch accidentally got peacock eggs from the farm supply instead of turkey eggs—don't ask, John's got a lot of things going on —and when the damned things hatched, they were defi-nitely not turkeys. Since all the chicks were male, he decided to keep 'em and make the best of it. He was gonna start that rental company I mentioned once the birds were old enough to grow tail feathers." I winced. "But it seems like Dave's lungs grew along with his train. He's gotten *loud*, and he kept squawking at John's dog—"

"That's odd. Peafowl aren't usually noisy outside of mating season," Lane said, holding the door open for me. "I wonder if the dog was scaring him."

"Maybe." I jogged down the steps and over to the side door of the garage. "But Dave's not supposed to be doing his tail feather thing outside of mating season either, and here we are. Maybe Dave's mating senses are going haywire, and he forgets what he's supposed to be looking for in a mate."

As soon as I opened the door, the bird in question began squawking at us. Within moments of catching sight of the gorgeous man behind me, Dave's tail feathers came whipping up too, spreading majestically like a magician waving a deck of fancy cards.

"Same, Dave," I muttered to the bird under my breath. "Same."

Lane took in the sight of the makeshift bird enclosure I'd created in the space. "You must have bought up all the baby gates in town."

I shook my head. "Nah. John picked 'em up at the Walmart over in Lafayette. It's the only way to keep them from messing with my tools."

I'd shoved all of my woodworking tools, machinery, and half-crafted Entwinin' wreaths to one side of the garage while the other half was now a peacock habitat.

"Wow." Lane ignored the birds, his gaze drawn to the Entwinin' wreath that lay on my workbench. It was nothing special yet—a simple twelve-inch wreath in the shape of a Celtic knot, just waiting for someone to take it and add their own special stamp with flowers or charms of some kind— but he seemed stunned. "You made this? For your festival? Is it... is it for someone special?"

"Well, yes... and no." I grinned. "The Entwinin' is a chance to show the most important person or people in your life that you love 'em. So I guess you might say that every person who receives a wreath is special to *someone*, but if you mean special to *me*, in a romantic kind of way? Nah. Never twined a vine for my own sweetheart before."

I'd actually never had a sweetheart to twine one for, if I

were being totally honest, but I worried that saying so might sound pathetic, so I hurried on.

"Giving a wreath's not always romantic—some folks give wreaths to their closest friends 'cause that kind of love's no less important—but it's always about creating something that symbolizes how much the relationship means to you. It's a real individual thing. The shape you choose matters, the type of wisteria branches you use matters—you gotta get the whippy ones for best results, and you can't get those late in the season—and the things you decorate it with matter too. It's supposed to be a labor of love. *But...*"

My grin turned wry. "The truth is, Lane, that there are lots more folks in the Thicket with love in their hearts than there are folks who can twine a vine. Not that anyone expects perfection, of course—the real perfection is the love that the maker has for their Entwined." I shrugged. "But nobody should have to lose a finger to a penknife just to show their love, so I always make up a bunch of extra wreaths for folks to decorate."

Lane looked like he might have some follow-up questions, but just then, Dave let out a mighty squawk that suggested he was not okay with being ignored.

I found myself laughing. "Keep your feathers on, Dave." I shook my head at Lane. "You can guess why John was a desperate man when he came to me this morning. The squawking is upsetting his wife and every animal at his place. Worst possible time for me to acquire new family members since the Entwinin' is coming up, and it's looking to be bigger than ever this year, but I agreed to take them all 'cause I couldn't separate Dave from his bros, you know? I put them in here because I didn't know if it was okay to leave them out in the cold." I gestured to the four animals making themselves at home in the musty space. "I asked my friend Diesel about it, but he keeps his chickens in a freaking palace, and I wouldn't be surprised if they had their own Netflix account. I'm not sure he's the best person to take advice from."

Lane climbed into the enclosure. "Well, peafowl are pretty hardy as far as the cold goes, but they'll want a roost. Even a broomstick or two-by-four mounted a few feet off the ground would work. They like to tuck their feet up under their breast to stay warm."

He approached the troublemaker, who was still hell-bent on shouting over us. "I can't believe I couldn't hear this from upstairs."

"Not yet, anyway. I think he's been getting louder since he got here," I said grimly. I pointed at the ceiling. "But I made sure the place was really well insulated before you moved in. I'd hate to disturb you."

Lane shot me a smile that was sweeter than any smile he'd ever given me. "You really would, wouldn't you?"

I lifted a shoulder in a half shrug. With Lane looking at me like that, the squirming feeling was back a hundredfold, and it was having all kinds of predictable results on me. "It's not that complicated," I said.

"No," he said softly. "I guess it's not."

I frowned, but Lane had already turned back to the peacocks. "These baby gates might discourage the peacocks from walking around, but you should know they can definitely fly over them if they want to. After tonight's cold weather, we might want to move them out back so they can roost in the oak tree. There are some branches on that one they'd love, and the backyard is fully fenced, right?"

I watched him squat down to inspect the screaming peacock. Lane's hands were gentle as he smoothed his fingers over the bird's body. "Dave seems bright. Obviously full of energy."

I grunted. "This *energy* is going to keep both of us up all night if he gets any louder."

Lane turned to smile at me over his shoulder. "If the insulation isn't enough, you could always try earplugs."

"Then I wouldn't be able to hear you if you need me," I said without thinking. As soon as the words were out of my mouth, I wished them back in. "I mean... heh. Not... not that you'd need *me*. I just meant, what if someone murdered you? Loudly? Or like... used a chainsaw? I've heard about that."

Lane's eyes had gotten progressively wider as my mouth had gone off on its little joy ride. "What if I'm *chainsaw massacred?*"

"That would *suck*," I emphasized.

Lane tilted his head at me, the edge of his lips quirking up a little. "Little bit."

I cleared my throat and looked around. "But I could get *you* earplugs. I think I have some in my workbench. Hold on."

I made my way past the piled-up scrap wood, the coils of dried wisteria vines, and other random shit until I was at my workbench with the packed shelves above. "Pretty sure they're in one of these Cool Whip containers."

Lane moved from one bird to the other, giving them all a cursory looking-over. "Stop, Jay. I can't accept your earplugs. What would I do if *you* were the one chainsaw massacred? I'd sleep right through it. Which isn't neighborly at all."

"I'd want you to sleep right through it! You don't get enough sleep as it is. And just imagine what a hellish day you'd wake up to. No. You need your sleep." I found the earplugs and shook out a few into my hand before piling the Cool Whip container back on the shelf.

Lane watched me pick my way back over to him. "I'd need my sleep on account of the...?"

I frowned at him. "Crime scene brouhaha. Emergency vehicles and whatnot. It would be a mess, I'd imagine. Here." I held out the earplugs, but he refused to take them. "Lane. Take them. You need your sleep. And this asshole's going to keep you up all night."

He met my eyes. When he spoke, his voice was softer. "Not sure I'd mind if this asshole kept me up all night, to be honest."

Tension sparked between us as I wondered if it was possible he was implying what I thought he was implying.

Me? *Me?*

"You..." I began. "Me... I... Wait. You think I'm an asshole?"

Lane opened his mouth to respond, but I quickly cut in. "Don't answer that. Stupid question. What person brings up a chainsaw massacre right before bedtime? An asshole, that's who. I didn't mean to make things weird. I just—" I stopped and ran my fingers through my hair. "Hell, I just—"

I didn't know what I *just.*

"Jay. Pretty sure I'm the asshole if you think I'd rather get my beauty sleep than help defend you from homicidal maniacs."

"I didn't say you'd *rather.* I said you *should,*" I corrected.

Lane stepped closer and held out a hand to me. I took it to help keep him steady while he climbed over the baby gates. The feel of his strong hand in mine made the little hairs on my arm prickle. "Doesn't neighborliness go both ways?" he asked. "Isn't it okay for you to expect people to give you the same consideration you give them?"

Once he was standing on my side of the gates, I couldn't bring myself to let go of his hand. "The peacock," I blurted, remembering we were here for a reason.

I noticed Lane didn't seem all that ready to let go of my hand either. "Your cock is fine," he said with a wink. "I think Dave's just out of sorts from being moved around. It happens. It could just mean that he's curious or that he's trying to display dominance. Peacocks need exercise and entertainment, which means we need to get them a roost and maybe some other things to occupy them. But it doesn't have to be tonight."

Lane's thumb slid over the back of my hand. "Oh," I breathed. "Good. Uh... thanks for taking a look. I was worried something was wrong with him."

The air crackled around us, broken periodically by the insistent cries of the peacock flaunting his wares behind the handsome veterinarian.

Lane continued, the curve of his lips almost flirty, if such a thing was possible. "Or maybe he just likes to show off for you. Maybe you were right earlier when you said his mating senses were going haywire. Sometimes a peacock wants what it wants." He grinned. "Even when it's not in mating season."

My stomach tumbled. I couldn't take my eyes off his lips. "I *do* like a man with plumage," I murmured.

He shifted and reached up to touch my chin, tilting my head back so my gaze naturally moved up from his lips to his eyes. "I don't think you're an asshole. The furthest thing from it, Jay. I was just making a bad joke earlier. I'm sorry."

I sucked in a breath. "No apologies necessary. I can definitely be an asshole sometimes."

Lane's eyes flicked back and forth as if studying me.

"You brought me soup when I was sick. Not an asshole move."

I swallowed. His nearness was making me dizzy. "Just a neighborly thing to do."

"You rehabilitated my reputation in town when I came off as grumpy and harried in the beginning. Not an asshole move."

I shrugged. "I could tell you were out of sorts. People only needed a chance to see the real you."

His hand moved from my chin to caress my cheek with the back of his fingers. "Jaybird. You chiseled ice off my car this morning and offered to put winter air in my tires. You're *not* an asshole."

I leaned into his touch and tried not to preen like the bird still flaunting behind him. "Sometimes it seems like you don't like me all that much. I worry maybe you—"

Lane lurched forward and pressed his lips against mine, shocking me enough to grunt in surprise. Maybe I shouldn't have been so shocked—he'd had his hand on my face, after all—but I was. My brain couldn't quite grasp how a beautiful, smart, successful man like Lane Desmond could want someone like me.

But—and this bore repeating—while I wasn't as smart as Lane, I definitely wasn't stupid. I kissed that man back for all I was worth.

My hands came around to press against his back, holding him close while my lips learned the shape of him. His mouth tasted like Italian Gentleman pasta—the food *I* had cooked for him—and that knowledge, combined with Lane's own sweetness, made the zesty Italian flavors extra delicious.

Lane's hands continued to cup my face as I pressed even closer, shifting my hardening cock against the bulge in the front of his soft pants. I silently cursed my thick jeans for keeping me from feeling more of him.

After a moment, my hands moved from his back down to his ass, and I cupped his cheeks with my hands. Lane pulled back enough to groan a curse. But instead of kissing me again, he pressed his forehead to mine.

"I like you, Jay," he said with a smile. "I like you a lot. You're just so damned *nice*."

It didn't sound like a criticism, exactly, but like something Lane couldn't quite comprehend, the same way I didn't understand some of the podcasts I'd heard him listening to... or how I'd come to be standing in my garage with his face touching mine.

I really, really hoped my niceness wasn't a dealbreaker for him... but just in case, I started arguing.

"I'm not nice. Not at all. In fact, just yesterday, I saw Mrs. Jackson—Hunter's mom—heading to the only open cashier at Henson's Grocery, and I deliberately picked up the pace to beat her there. She had at least twenty cans of diced tomatoes on account of the buy-one-get-one thing they still have going on, and if you know Sherri Wattel at all, you know she'd insist on scanning every single one of them through."

Lane's laughter rumbled out of his chest. "Wow. You're going to hell, Jaybird Proud."

"Yep." I nodded eagerly. "Sure am. Of course, Mrs. Jackson and I got to talking, and she asked me to help her out to her car with her bags, so I ended up spending half an hour watching Sherri ring the cans anyway," I admitted. "But... but that's not all! I also deliberately didn't clean out Hector Moore's ashtray in his truck at the car wash the other day."

Lane whistled, low and impressed. "Oh, well, now,

that's *terrible*," he said, sounding so happy and fond I kept talking.

"Right? I mean, technically, it's because Hector knows how I feel about his smoking. I warned him he was gonna have to clean his own butts from now on, kinda hoping it would help him kick the habit, but he still looked *real* disappointed."

"Mmhm." Lane rubbed his nose against mine.

I racked my brain, trying to think of something even worse that I'd done. When I took a deep breath and inhaled Lane's scent, the answer came to me.

"Not only that, but I got a call asking for old coat donations... and I didn't donate, even though I do, in fact, have an old coat right now." I nodded once, firmly, because that ought to convince him. It had been a purely selfish choice on my part. Not nice at *all*.

But Lane only seemed tickled pink by my admission... which kinda concerned me.

Was he evil?

When he pulled back and smirked—the man was unlawfully good-looking, especially when his eyes twinkled like that—I decided I didn't care if he was. Evil looked real good on him.

"There was a perfectly good, *nice* reason you chose not to donate your coat, wasn't there?" he teased. "Go on. Admit it."

I narrowed my eyes. "I'd prefer more kissing to this interrogation, thank you very much."

"I'll kiss you for every evil deed you tell me about. Howbout that?"

"Mfh."

He chuckled, and the sound made my stomach fizz like soda pop. "Tell me why you didn't donate the coat, Jay."

I realized I was stuck. I either had to lie to someone I never wanted to lie to... or I had to reveal something embarrassing.

If given the choice between hurting him and humoring him, I'd have to choose humor every time. So I confessed the truth.

"Because it's the one I brought you that day you left yours at home, and it still smells like you."

Chapter Three

Lane

Jᴀʏ's ᴡᴏʀᴅs lingered in the air between us.

It still smells like you.

No human could be this sweet. Not without a reason. Not without a... a motive.

But my brain immediately called up a million examples of how he could be—how he *was*—and played them for me like one of those cheesy but adorable movie montages.

Last summer, when I'd planned to spend a whole afternoon relaxing in the backyard, I'd gotten derailed by some pictures on Chad's Instagram and had instead spent hours hate-scrolling his honeymoon pictures, wondering what the hell was wrong with me. I hadn't realized I'd said the words out loud until suddenly, Jay was beside me with a giant pair of clippers, asking for my help while he trimmed back the sickly crepe myrtle behind the garage.

"This little tree's a tricky one," he'd said as he'd worked. "If left to its own devices, it'll tangle itself up until it blocks out its own sunlight." He'd shot me a sideways glance. "But there's nothing wrong with it that a little pruning won't fix."

By the time we'd finished gardening—which had taken a

lot longer than necessary since Jay had "accidentally" squirted me with the hose during cleanup—I'd forgotten all about Chad.

Another time last fall, after I'd spent a full day and night at the clinic trying to save the life of Maisy Topher's seventeen-year-old German shepherd, Claude—"*He's my best friend, Doc Lane. Please.*"—I'd arrived home shortly after sunrise to find Jay sitting on my steps holding a takeout container of triple chocolate cake from Annie's Bakery.

He'd chattered at me for a while—some story about them giving away the cake on a two-for-one special, so it would have been wrong not to take both pieces but also wrong to *eat* both pieces, and would I mind solving this ethical dilemma for him?—while I'd sat silently beside him on the steps, shoving cake into my mouth and feeling a little less bone-weary.

Then, a month or so ago, Jay had stopped by the clinic to warn me there was a snowstorm coming and not to work too late. I remembered he'd been dressed up—black slacks and a crisp white button-down shirt, topped with a brown dress coat instead of his usual blue parka.

"Why you so fancy today, Jaybird?" Alva had asked.

He'd frowned. "Mrs. Herring needed a ride to the funeral home. I didn't expect they'd appreciate my showing up in blue jeans."

"I'm sorry," I'd murmured, not knowing who Mrs. Herring was or who she'd lost.

He'd snorted lightly. "Don't be. Mr. Herring was awful. She's better off without him, to be honest. We all are."

Alva had nodded firmly but silently, making the entire situation extremely awkward.

"Well, uh... thanks for the warning about the snow. I do have a couple of late appointments, but I'll be careful."

Jay's lips had turned down in a scowl. "Surely you can cancel them. Your vehicle doesn't have winter tires."

In the end, I'd somehow been left with Jay's four-wheel-drive truck, his dress coat, and a dozen hot chicken tenders in a brown paper bag. I remembered staring at the door for a full minute after the coatless man had absconded with my vehicle and left me with a warm meal.

Alva had let out a breath before heading back to the lab. "You've been Jaybirded, yes you have."

Despite all the experience I'd had with the man up to that point, I still hadn't understood what she'd meant. I'd expected Jay to be put out or annoyed. At the very least, for him to act like I'd owed him a favor.

He hadn't.

He'd greeted me with a relieved "Howdy, neighbor" when I'd returned home that day, exchanged keys with no fuss, and ushered me up the freshly swept steps to my apartment with a friendly "Keep warm!" He'd never referred to the incident again.

I looked at Jay now, red-lipped and handsome as always. Only this time, he was red-lipped from kissing me, and his handsome was exponentially more compelling since I'd tasted the man's mouth.

What was I supposed to be doing?

Oh, right. Kissing him for each of his evil, evil deeds.

Except now, *finally*, I was starting to think I understood him.

"You're obsessed with looking out for people," I murmured before leaning in to give him the kiss I'd promised.

"I guess, a little." His arms came around me again, and the feel of his big, strong hands firm against my back made me groan. "One person in particular, though..."

My heart pounded. "Why me?" I whispered.

Jay's face was serious. "You're in high need, Dr. Lane. I've never met a man who needed taking care of the way you do."

The laugh spilled out of me. "I do not. I'll have you know I managed to survive many, many years without the help of Jaybird Proud."

"Survived," he repeated like he was considering the word. "I guess so." Jay's hand came up to stroke my jaw with his thumb. The expression on his face could only be described as *fond*... and I was pretty sure I was looking at him the same way.

In addition to making me feel cared for, this man made me feel noticed and seen. He always had, though I'd been too busy trying to puzzle out his motives to realize it until that moment.

To be honest, it was a little overwhelming.

If Jay *really* saw me, did he see all the same flaws Chad had seen? Did he realize he'd been displaying his feathers, so to speak, for a man given to "emotional evasion," who was "indifferent" toward relationships? Did he recognize what a bad bet I was?

In that moment, with my heartbeat thudding in my temples and my belly tight with want, I reminded myself that nobody had said a word about relationships. I could see in his eyes that Jaybird Proud wanted me, and the man was too sexy to ignore.

Not to mention, I hadn't gotten laid in a very, very long time.

"Here's another evil deed for you, Lane. I used bottled Italian seasoning tonight because I ran out of fresh basil."

"No!" I gasped, recoiling back in mock horror. "I've been defrauded of my authentic Italian Gentleman experience! I've been cheated. I demand my money back! Oh... wait."

He smirked. "Not only that, but remember that time I needed you to spot me on the ladder because I was feeling wobbly?"

I remembered holding his hips from behind while he reached to replace a lightbulb in the floodlight on the corner of the garage. The feel of his body heat through his jeans and the sight of his stellar ass cheeks right in front of my face meant not only did I remember, but I'd also imagined many, many other endings to that simple task.

Jay must have seen the heat in my eyes because his smile got wider. "I wasn't wobbly. Well, if I was, it was because you were so damned close and looked hot as fuck in your doctor's coat. I just wanted you closer."

I leaned in to tease his lips with mine. "You *are* evil. Imagine taking advantage of an unsuspecting neighbor in such a way. For shame, Jay. For *shame*."

This time, the kiss started off playful but soon intensified.

Jay was more aggressive than I'd known he could be, and it was hot as hell. Despite his adorable, insecure bumbling around me, when he put his hands on me, he was plenty confident. And because he was bigger and stronger than I was, his physical confidence made me harder than ever. I imagined him manhandling me in bed, moving me where he wanted me, and then pounding me into the nearest surface with all that brute strength.

Chad had been meticulous about keeping trim, to the point he sometimes seemed like a carefully curated collection of bones. But Jay? He was muscular and fit from working with his body all day, every day. He was not afraid of a carb, soft drinks, or dairy products. In fact, I'd once seen him make himself sick on cotton candy after buying a cotton candy machine to use at one of the town festivals. "Gotta test it out before giving any to the kids, Lane," he'd said with a bright pink grin.

"Come upstairs with me," I said now, pulling away after the peacock cried his displeasure once again.

Jay's hands had made their way down to my ass, and now they cupped it possessively. "I don't want to take my hands off you."

I met his eyes. "Okay, but I was planning on getting naked upstairs."

Jay grabbed my hand, shut off all but one low light in the garage, and yanked me up the stairs to my place. I had half a second to wonder where the sweet, sometimes reserved man I'd come to know had been hiding this take-charge side of himself... and then we were upstairs, and he was looking at me with unbridled heat in his eyes, and I decided I was *very* on board with Jaybird having hidden depths.

"Clothes off," he grunted as soon as my apartment door was closed behind us.

"I didn't even know you were gay until today," I said, yanking off the hoodie and tee and tossing them both on the nearby love seat.

The look on his face was comical as he hopped around, toeing off his boots. "Lane," he admonished. "How could you not know? I've undressed you with my eyes every day for six months."

Knowing he'd been admiring my body for that long made my face flush. Suddenly, all those "neighborly" things he'd been doing for me took on a different meaning. I didn't want to admit that I'd been too distracted by his sleeveless shirts and football knowledge to come to what should have been a very logical conclusion, though, so I blurted, "Why didn't you say something?"

"Say what? 'I won't charge you rent, but I do want to fuck you'? Pretty sure that's illegal, baby, even in Tennessee."

I moved over to help him with the button and zipper on his jeans. "You could have found a middle ground. Maybe complimented me on my hair or something."

Jay's confusion was clear. "Lane. The first day I met you, I said you were hot as fuck."

The memory of that day was hazy, mostly because we'd been pouring sweat from dragging my shit up the stairs on a day when the heat was sweltering. "I thought you said *it* was hot as fuck! The weather. Jesus."

"Yeah, well, that too. And you don't pack light, no offense." He pulled off his T-shirt and dropped it on the floor, exposing his nipples to the cool air.

I ran my hands up his torso, the dark hair rough against my fingertips, until I could feel his hardening nipples. His stomach muscles contracted as he sucked in a breath. "I couldn't believe you volunteered to help me unload the truck."

Jay's hands moved down to yank at the drawstring of my lounge pants. I wasn't wearing any underwear, so when he tugged on the front, he got an eyeful down the front of them. "Can we stop talking now? My brain is making Disco Dave noises."

He stepped closer and pushed my lounge pants down, eying my cock hungrily the entire time. As the pants fell to the ground, so did Jay.

When his knees hit the carpet, he grasped my shaft and glanced up at me. "Okay?"

I nodded as the sound of my jagged breathing seemed to

fill the room. My fingers sifted through his untamed hair as his gaze moved down to my erection.

"Want this so fucking much," he murmured, almost to himself.

I tried not to wonder who else he'd done this with here in town. Had he ever hooked up with his friend Hunter? Or Dunn Johnson? Or Diesel? The town was full of beautiful gay men, and the thought of any of them with Jay made my stomach ache.

As soon as his hot tongue wrapped around the head of my cock, though, my jealous imaginings popped like a thin bubble floating past a porcupine.

"Fuck," I groaned.

Jay's big hands clutched my hips and moved around to grab my ass. As he teased me with his mouth, he grinned up at me. "You have a killer ass. Always wanted to touch it. And, uh... stuff."

I ran a thumb across his wet lips. "And stuff? Jaybird Proud, are you saying you want to fuck me?"

His smile dropped, and his eyes heated. "More than anything."

As his mouth covered my cock again, I wondered what it would feel like to be pounded into the mattress by this sexy sweetheart. He might be strong and confident in some ways, but he was still so incredibly eager to please.

"Oh fuck," I gasped as the tip of his tongue pressed against just the right spot. My hands tightened in his hair. "Just like that."

He cupped my sac and ran a strong finger behind it, pressing against my taint and watching my eyes for my reaction. Since my brain was still swimming in the notion of being fucked by the man, his fingers and mouth had an easy job of it. Within moments, I felt like I was on the knife's edge of coming.

"Bed," I cried, grasping my last rational thought. "Want to suck you too."

"You don't have to," he said hoarsely. "This time can just be about you."

The man was so selfless, even in this. But I wanted to give him pleasure as much as I wanted to take it.

"Jay," I said more insistently. "Bed. Now."

We scrambled up onto my bed, ditching the last of our clothes until we were a tangled mass of body parts. Jay's head was quickly buried between my thighs while I got my first glimpse of his fat cock.

I breathed out a curse and brought the tip to my lips to kiss it and bathe it with my lips and tongue. The deep sound Jay made in response caused my balls to tighten. His hands moved all over me as we sucked each other off, and just as I was ready to shoot, one of his fingertips ghosted over my hole.

"Fuck," I cried, pulling off his cock and jacking him erratically as my orgasm hit. I arched into his mouth and felt his fingers clutch at my ass as he swallowed me down. As soon as I could, I put my mouth back on him to bring him the kind of pleasure he'd given me.

When his orgasm hit, he shouted and turned his face into my inner thigh, kissing it and moaning into my skin as his release landed hot and salty on my tongue.

I swallowed quickly and cleaned him up with my tongue before pulling away and leaning back on the bed to catch my breath.

It took me a minute to notice the tiny kitten-like kisses he continued to press into the tender skin of my inner thigh.

It was so fucking sweet, something not many men had ever done to me before.

I moved around until I lay half on top of him so I could kiss his mouth again.

Jay was an incredible kisser, attentive and considerate. We kissed lazily for a long time, legs pretzeled together and spent cocks slack against each other's damp skin. Jay's hands moved reverently over my back and ass, partway down the back of my thighs, and up into my hair, as if he wanted to touch as much of me as he could. "So gorgeous," he murmured against my skin. "So hot."

I shivered at the sensation, and my cock tried to rally.

Had anyone ever been so focused on me after sex? I didn't think so. I sure as hell hadn't enjoyed it this much.

This was the part of hookups that so often turned awkward, in my experience. I wanted nothing more than to lie there in the afterglow, to soak up all of those kisses and touches, but I was pretty sure I was supposed to do something to wrap it up, to confirm it was just a hookup and definitely nothing serious. After all, Jay was such a considerate person he was likely to stick around to keep from hurting my feelings, and I didn't want him to feel obligated.

Jay must have felt some change in my body, a tensing of my muscles as I prepared to disengage.

"I'm not leaving," he murmured against my mouth.

"Oh." I blinked. Was he a mind reader? "Good," I heard myself say, surprised to find I meant it.

He pulled back and met my eyes. "I know you don't want anything serious, but I..." He swallowed. "I want to sleep here with you tonight. It doesn't have to mean anything."

I didn't know exactly what I *wanted*, but I was pretty sure I knew what was *possible*. Nothing had changed in the last hour, after all. I was still shitty at relationships at the best of times, and Jay and I were still incredibly different people. But I couldn't help asking, "What makes you think I don't want anything serious?"

Jay's eyebrows winged up. "Do you?"

"N-no!" I shook my head fervently. "God, no. Nope. Noooo. I mean, I just got out of a relationship. Er, well, a year ago. Six months before I moved here. And it ended badly. Chad didn't... I wasn't..." I took a deep breath and let it out. "So... no."

His eyebrows settled. "Right. So. It's just... casual... whatever. Yeah?"

Logically, I knew he was correct, so even though something about his words felt wrong—jarringly wrong—I ignored it. I forced myself to say, "Yeah. Good. Casual."

He leaned in to kiss me again. I lost myself in the overwhelming feel of him, the intoxicating press of his strong body against mine. The warmth of his skin and the sounds of his enjoyment.

We kissed for what seemed like hours, eventually stroking each other off when the intensity ratcheted up. After cleaning up the mess, we fell against each other again to catch our breaths.

And when the morning came, I expected things to get very awkward very quickly.

Except... they didn't.

Jay appeared at my bedside in his underwear and holding two mugs of coffee. "Scooch over. It's cold as balls out here."

I moved over without thinking and felt the icy draft he brought with him as he returned to the warmth of the bed. As I took the hot mug from him, he settled against the headboard. "Okay, tell me what the peacocks need, and I'll get it fixed up for them. You said something about a roost, right?"

"Yes. You're really sweet," I said softly. "Not a lot of people would care so much."

Jay shrugged like he was uncomfortable with the praise. "I like taking care of things, like you said. I don't always know the best way to do it, but I'm a quick learner. And what's so wrong with wanting to make people... or, like, peacocks, I guess... happy, when it makes me happy too?"

"Not a single thing."

He looked at me for a moment like he was trying to decide if I was being sincere or just telling him what he wanted to hear. Then, his face split in a wide grin. "Good. 'Cause I might not have set out to acquire a flock of peacocks, but they're mine now. And I take care of what's mine."

I sucked in a breath. *What would it be like to be his?* I couldn't help wondering.

But then I stopped myself. There was no use wondering about impossible things.

We spent the next half hour discussing proper peacock habitats, the fifteen minutes after that sucking each other off in a shared shower, and then separated to go back to our real lives.

Except it wasn't quite that easy. Even when I was supposed to be concentrating on my work, I kept remembering how it had felt to be touched by Jay, adored by him. I already knew what it felt like to have him care for me in a "neighborly" way, but having him in my bed was an entirely different thing. The orgasm had been phenomenal, but the way he'd focused on me afterward and insisted on staying with me was—

"But those anal glands are all yours."

"Huh?" I snapped my head up to see Pete Winchell, our vet tech, glaring at me.

"Are you even here today, Doc Lane? Because I said your name, like, ten times and then had to threaten you with an impacted anal gland to get you to pay attention."

I rubbed my eyes and glanced down at the exam table. Buttercup's gaze was reproachful.

"Sorry," I said, aiming my apology to both Pete and the dog. "I was daydreaming, I guess. My bad."

"Uh-huh." Pete raised one eyebrow. "So who's the guy? Is he hot? And does he have a twin brother, close single friend, or heartbroken ex in need of a shoulder to cry on?" He wiggled his eyebrows meaningfully. "'Cause I've got sturdy shoulders, and I wanna say I'm not that desperate, but... I might be that desperate."

I felt my face go hot. "I said nothing about a... anyone. I have no idea what you're talking about."

"No?" Pete pursed his lips. "If that's the story you wanna go with, okaaaay... I'll just have to tell everyone I caught you smiling goofily and daydreaming about expressing Buttercup's glands."

I shot him an exasperated look. "You don't *have* to tell anyone anything at all since it's none of their business."

He gave me a pitying smile. "That's not how it works in the Thicket, Doc. Everybody here knows everybody else. And that's a wonderful thing because it means everyone looks out for each other and really cares. But even a CIA agent couldn't keep a secret here."

Buttercup the dog let out a sigh that echoed my own.

I shook it off and managed to focus—or, more accurately, tried to fake it and failed—for the rest of the day.

When it was finally time to go home, I decided to stop

by the new noodle restaurant in town, Hot Noods, and pick up dinner for Jay to pay him back for the pasta.

When I pulled into the driveway, I saw a pair of sawhorses set up by the garage with several two-by-fours on them. Next to the lumber was a chop saw and a haphazard pile of tools. It was clear Jay had moved the peacocks out into the backyard, as we'd discussed, and that he was working on their habitat, even though it was mostly dark and pretty cold out.

As I got out of the car, grabbing the takeout bag, Jay stepped into the open door of the garage and peered out. He reached up, bracing his hands on the overhang of the garage in a way that seemed deliberately designed to make the biceps popping out of his sleeveless shirt ripple and a mouth-watering slice of abs appear above the waistband of his jeans. He gave me a deliberate up-down look that made my mouth water and my cock plump behind my scrub pants.

"Well. Howdy, neighbor," he said, injecting his voice with more of a sleepy drawl than usual.

I sucked in a breath and nearly choked on my own spit.

"H-hi," I said, then scowled at my own ridiculousness.

I was a thirty-mumble-year-old man who'd had sex with many people. Like, *many*. There was no reason for me to feel like a middle schooler with his first crush just because Jaybird and I had hooked up.

We'd said casual, for God's sake.

I cleared my throat. "I, uh... picked up some noodles. For... dinner?" I lifted the bag slightly.

Jay's gaze dropped to the bag, and his forehead creased. "Oh." His arms dropped, and he nodded. "Sure. Yeah. I won't hold you up. Their wontons are the best, but you can't eat 'em cold."

I blinked. "No, Jay, I meant I got noodles for both of us. In case you wanted to, you know... come up and eat with me?"

My breathy voice managed to turn the simple invitation into the world's silliest innuendo.

Smooth, Lane. Stop talking.

But the way Jay stared at me, still frowning, made me think maybe I needed to talk even more.

"I just... I thought... I can't cook for shit, but I know you love their stuff, and I wanted to do something nice for you, so..." I pressed my lips together, stopping my babble.

For a person trying to keep things casual, I was sounding the exact opposite, damn it.

"You got me dinner?" Jay said, sounding as thrilled and befuddled as if I'd offered him a billion dollars, tax-free.

Now, it was my turn to look confused. "Well, yeah. You've been feeding me for, like, six months," I teased. "It's about time, right?"

Jay grinned and walked toward me slowly like I was an animal he didn't want to startle. He didn't seem to realize that I was more likely to sprout wings and fly than I was to walk away when he was looking at me with heat and appreciation in his eyes.

He took the bag from my hand, and slowly, leaving me plenty of time to move away, he pressed a soft kiss to my lips. "Thanks, Lane. And... just so I understand... will there be a *dessert* component to dinner?"

"Yeah." I started to say there were cookies in the bag when I realized that "dessert" actually *was* an innuendo.

Jesus.

I immediately shut my mouth and flushed hot all over. "I mean, yes. I... I had a lot of fun last night. There's no reason we can't do that again, right? Casually, I mean?"

"Casually," he repeated. He stepped closer so that our chests were pressed together, dipped his face to my neck, inhaled deeply, and groaned. "Fuck, you smell good. Can we eat dessert first?"

I couldn't imagine how that was true, given the day I'd had, but I didn't argue. Instead, I grabbed his hand and towed him, laughing, up the stairs to my apartment.

Two nights in a row didn't make a casual thing not-casual, I told myself firmly. It was simply enjoying a thing while it lasted.

A sentiment I repeated to myself for the next couple of months.

Chapter Four

Jay

EVERY ONCE IN A WHILE, as I was going through my regular life in the Thicket—like while I was giving a Corolla a particularly fine wax or helping Grandma Emmaline with her latest artistic endeavor (a larger-than-life mural of her husband, Amos, clothed only in a loincloth)—it would hit me that I, plain old Jaybird Proud, was keeping time with gorgeous, funny, supremely talented Lane Desmond.

I got to touch him.

I got to kiss him.

I got to watch his gorgeous body kneeling at my feet and sucking my cock on the regular.

I got to hear the pretty little cries he made whenever my hands were on him.

I got to see his eyes go unfocused when he came for me.

I got to catalog his shy blushes while I cleaned him up.

And best of all, I got to take care of him.

Not that I hadn't taken care of Lane even before we were sleeping together, of course. As he'd pointed out more than once, taking care of folks was what I liked to do. But now, I didn't bother holding back... though I still tried to keep it subtle since I figured Lane didn't want to take our relationship public.

That was why I was determined to play it cool when I walked into the vet clinic one February morning.

"Hi, Jay. He has two more surgeries before lunch," Pete said without looking up from the computer behind the reception desk.

I glanced around the empty waiting area and then out onto the street, where pedestrians strolled past the window as they did their morning errands.

"How'd you know it was me without looking?" I asked suspiciously. "I could've been Rosario Cockburn with his pet rat. I could have been Halle Jorgensen bringing in Veronica. I could have been Diesel and Mari bringing in Elsa the chicken." I named four of the people I'd seen passing by. "I could've been anyone."

Petey pursed his lips and nodded as if considering this.

"Well... I figured you weren't Rosario because Punkin was just here yesterday for his checkup. I figured you weren't Halle because Veronica the ball python was here at the same time as Punkin, and there was almost... ahem... an incident—"

My jaw dropped. "Damn. The circle of life played out right here in the waiting room?"

Petey rolled his eyes. "I said *almost*. But mostly, Jay, I knew it was you because it's 10:57 a.m."

"Uh... okay." I frowned. "So?"

"So, sometimes around this time, you've heard a report on the news about a flood in Florida and want to make sure Lane's got his boots, just in case the flooding spreads north. Sometimes around this time, you have a burning question, like needing to know Lane's middle name—"

"Because I'm his landlord," I said firmly. "It was important for me to know that he's Lane *Bryan* Desmond for legal purposes."

"And most of the time," Petey went on like he hadn't heard me, "right around eleven, you get concerned about Lane's blood sugar, and you bring him a snack."

"I wouldn't say it's *most* of the time," I muttered.

But then I thought about it. *Was* it most of the time?

"Remember last week, when you claimed you'd just *happened* to find an entire peanut butter sandwich in your pocket, despite you not liking peanut butter?"

"That..." My face went a little hot. "That was a strange coincidence, I grant you. But Lane loves peanut butter, and it would have been wasteful—"

"Uh-huh." Petey waved a hand, eyes on his computer. "So leave your cookies, or umbrella, or sweater, or lunch, or whatever the heck you're bringing him today over there, and I'll get it to him when he has a break." He nodded over his shoulder toward the end of the high counter.

I sauntered over and casually slid several small packages of carrot sticks and Oreo cookies onto the counter.

Petey snorted.

"It's not... I mean... I just thought... if anyone was hungry... I know you and Lane work awfully hard, so—"

Just then, Lane came hustling out of the back, staring down at his phone. "Pete, call Stef Holmes and let her know Fluffernutter will be ready for pickup at—" He came to a halt as he caught sight of me and smiled sweetly. "Hey."

Did that smile make me look as goofy as I felt? "Howdy, neighbor."

"These two," Pete muttered before typing the customer's number into the phone keypad.

"Everything... okay?" Lane asked. His cheeks had turned a dusty crimson that made my stomach tighten.

"Oh, sure. Yeah. I was just..." I stopped and shuffled my feet. "In the neighborhood and thought I'd drop off some snacks. You know, in case you had any peckish... clients. Not a big deal." I gestured to the snack packs on the counter. "Anyway, I'll be on my way now."

"Wait, uh... wait." Lane hesitated and then glanced at the snacks as if trying to figure out what he wanted to say. "Carrots! That's strange, I was just craving carrots last night."

Now, I was the one shuffling my feet. "Were you? Huh. I hadn't noticed," I lied. "I just grabbed whatever was closest."

"Fucking Christ," Pete muttered.

"Hey, Lane, are you—oh!" Alva came out of the back, pulling on her white coat. Her eyes lit up when she saw the Oreos. "Snack time!" She twisted her wrist and checked her watch. "I hadn't realized it was eleven already."

This entire situation was cringe, and it reminded me of why I was never going to be the kind of guy Lane Desmond could be proud of. I had absolutely no chill.

"Gotta go," I said before bolting for the door.

Lane called after me again, but I didn't stop. Things were too good between us to risk fucking it up by saying something stupid in front of Lane's coworkers.

Or something *more* stupid, anyway.

I just... liked being with the man, that was all. And the hours between leaving him in the morning and greeting him in the garage tended to drag. I'd end up thinking about how good it felt to kiss him, and wishing I could see the smile on his face.

I worried sometimes that things were getting too good. Too... serious, at least on my part. And that was a problem.

Even though I'd lived in the Thicket my whole life and

there was no place I'd rather be, I'd learned pretty early on that folks—well, men—didn't want *serious* from me. They wanted a fun night, a few laughs, and some screaming orgasms.

It had never bothered me much since I hadn't been after anything serious myself, but with Lane...

"What the fuck is wrong with you?" Dunn Johnson asked when I slunk into the Partridge Pit to pick up some ribs after finishing my shift at the Suds Barn.

If Lane didn't want me turning up on his doorstep with food, I could at least deliver it to his doorstep before he returned home. That way, I'd still ensure he was properly fed after his long workday, and he wouldn't have to see me or feel obligated to give me a pity invite inside.

"Nothing's wrong, why?"

Dunn lifted his boot and used it to shove out the chair opposite him at one of the wooden tables. "You look miserable. Bad day at work? Tell Uncle Dunn all about it."

I threw myself down in the chair with a sigh. Dunn's husband, Tucker, eyed the two of us as he approached with a couple of cups full of icy-cold sweet tea. "Hey, Jay. You hungry? Want to join us for an early dinner?"

I shook my head. "Nah. Just put in an order for some ribs for later. How's it going at work? Ms. Vienna came by the car wash with her station wagon the other day and said things have been busy on account of the flu going around the school. I figured you've been run off your feet."

Dunn waved his hand to keep Tucker from answering. "He's fine. Flu's normal this time of year. Stop changing the subject. How's that fussbudget new vet?"

I stared at him in shock. "Lane Desmond is the furthest thing from a fussbudget! He's a... a... he's a... damn it, *what is the opposite of fussbudget?*"

"Nonchalant?" Tucker suggested. "Easygoing? Relaxed? Carefree?"

I stared at him, and he blushed. "Sorry. I, uh... I like crosswords."

The look Dunn gave him was so filled with love and pride I had to look away. "He's being modest. Tucker Johnson knows more words than anybody."

Tucker's blush intensified. "Drink your tea and hush," he said fondly. "Anyway, you like Lane just fine. You brought Bernadette to see him." To me, he explained, "That's about the highest compliment Dunn can pay a person."

Dunn made a grumbling noise. "The man called her my *pet*, Tucker, when anyone knows a pig is *livestock*."

Tucker nodded and pushed his glasses up. "I know, baby. But I think Lane was confused when you mentioned that Bernie sleeps in the house, under the dining room table."

"Only sometimes," Dunn scoffed. "Like for safety, when it's storming." He frowned. "Or when she seems lonely. Or when there are new episodes of *Bridgerton*. But otherwise, she's out in her pen. Which I told him."

"You did," Tucker agreed. "You sure did. But I think... I think maybe when you explained that there was running water in the pen and that you'd taught Bernie to operate the lever in case she needed a shower, that might have increased the confusion—"

"Pffft. That's just responsible livestock ownership."

"—and when you explained the part about how you had us draw up wills and list Parrish and Diesel as her guardians if something should happen to both of us... well, I can see where Lane's confusion came from, that's all I'm saying."

"We agreed we need someone we know will administer

her trust correctly." Dunn grabbed Tucker's hand. "But that doesn't make her a *pet*, Tuck. That'd be silly."

"You're absolutely right," Tucker soothed. He laid his free hand atop Dunn's. "The more I think about it, I can't imagine where Lane got that idea."

"Well, I'm sure Lane was just doing his job and taking care of his client," I said, a bit more hotly than maybe I should have. "He's an *excellent* vet and a good man. A great man. The *best* man." I glared at him.

Dunn raised one brow at me, his grievances seemingly forgotten. "Oh, *reeeeally*? Tell me more."

Tucker shot a look at Dunn and wiggled their joined hands. "No. Stand down, Cindy Ann."

Dunn's eyes twinkled with humor, but he didn't look away from me as he responded to his man. "I'm not my mother. And even if I was, that's hardly an insult. Cindy Ann Johnson is a saint on Earth."

Tucker and I exchanged a look. Dunn's mother, Cindy Ann, was a lovely, kind woman... and possibly the biggest matchmaker and gossip east of the Mississippi.

"But we aren't talking about her," Dunn continued. "We're talking about Doc Nonchalant." He grinned. "He's cute, your doc. Not, like, Tucker-cute, but cute."

I felt my face get hot... not because of anything related to the conversation, of course. Barbecue restaurants in general were overheated. It was a side effect of good brisket. "He's not mine."

"No?" Dunn took a slow swallow of sweet tea while continuing to study me. "I thought the guy was staying over your garage?"

Tucker nodded. "Isn't he your tenant? We thought he moved in after Charlie moved out."

"He is, but..." I shook my head. "What's that got to do with anything?"

"You're his landlord, so I figure you know him better than most. And there are all kinds of new guys moving into town now that Champ is expanding his security company. We might need to set him up."

Tucker rolled his eyes behind his glasses and fake-coughed the words, *Cindy Ann*. Dunn ignored him.

I inhaled slowly to keep from snapping. "Far as I know, Lane's not dating anyone," I said. "Not... not *seriously*, anyway. Probably wants a smart guy. Someone in... in management or something."

Dunn's teasing grin faded. "What do you mean? This guy a snob?" He shot Tucker a look. "See? This is what comes of people calling livestock *pets*."

"Hush, baby." Tucker reached over and massaged Dunn's shoulder. "Dunn's sensitive about these things. He wants to make sure you're being respected."

"Respected?" I glanced back and forth between them. "I don't get it."

"When Dunn and I got together, some folks—not anyone close to us, but *some* folks—wondered if we'd be a good match," Tucker explained. "They figured we're too different."

Dunn snorted. "'Cause I'm so shit with words that I can't do the *New York Times* crossword, even on a Monday, and 'cause Tucker gets trampled when he tries to help me get the cows into the milking pen. Such bullshit. We were best-best friends for years because our hearts are the same, no matter how different our lives are on the outside, and I fell in love with Tucker before I even realized I wasn't straight. If love can conquer *that*, let me tell you, it can conquer anything."

Tucker's eyes looked a little shiny. "You're fucking *great* with words when it counts, Dunn Johnson," he said fiercely. He cleared his throat. "But we're getting sidetracked. We were talking about Jay and Doc Lane."

"Nope. No. We weren't. There's no me and Doc Lane!" I insisted because it was true, even if I wished it weren't. "We're friendly. Landlord and tenant. It's totally... totally normal. Normal as can be. Like, Norm. Al."

The two of them exchanged a look before Dunn pulled a clean paper napkin out of the wooden box on the table. He pointed to the blank surface. "This right here is a list of all the times someone said something was normal when it was actually normal."

I closed my eyes and took a breath. "No, really. Can we change the subject, please? Brickle McNair—you know, the sheriff's deputy—came through the car wash today with a Jeep covered in camellia blossoms. Do you know the only camellia in town that's in bloom right now? It's the one at Jessica Greely's house." I bounced my eyebrows, waiting for them to process the juiciest piece of Thicket gossip to come out of the car wash in days.

Tucker looked confused. "Camellias aren't blooming this time of year. What gives?"

"That's not the point," I said at the same time Dunn pointed out Jessica's camellia was located by her garage... which happened to be her brother's grow house.

"The lights in there would be enough to keep my farm in bloom all winter in addition to his marijuana plants," he muttered.

"Exactly," I said, laughing. "So. Jessica and Brickle. Now, *there's* a romance, huh? Talk about star-crossed lovers. I really hope those crazy kids manage to make it work—"

"You want him," Tucker said softly. "You want Doc Lane."

"You *want* him!" Dunn said much more loudly. Several people turned their heads to stare. I scooted down in my seat and studied the blank napkin list again in hopes of finding one instance where normal meant normal.

No luck.

Tucker reached out and patted my hand like a little old lady. "How can we help?"

I shrugged and admitted, "You can't, Tucker. I meant what I said. Lane Desmond is above my pay grade. He's got fancy diplomas and knows shit I'll never know. Hell, the man reads books on self-help stuff. I work at a car wash. I graduated from Thicket High by the skin of my teeth."

Dunn's eyebrows jammed together. "Only because you were busy caring for your mom. And there's nothing wrong with working at a car wash, Jay." He lowered his voice and met my eyes. "Especially when you *own* said car wash."

I gaped at him. The Suds Barn ownership was a carefully guarded secret. I'd gone to great lengths over the years to imply that I ran it on behalf of an absentee out-of-towner. "Own it?" I asked, feigning ignorance.

Dunn rolled his eyes. "Fine. You want to play it that way, we can play it that way. But know this: I'm a farmer. My partner is a doctor. Am I below his pay grade? No, I'm not. Know why? Because I'm smart in other ways. I know all kinds of shit he doesn't know. And even if I didn't, do you think Tucker Johnson would love me less?"

I glanced at Tucker, who was looking at his husband with giant saucer eyes full of affection. "Er, no?"

"Correct. He loves me because of who I am right here," he said, banging his fist in the center of his torso.

"That's your pancreas, baby," Tucker murmured. Dunn

moved his fist up and banged again. "Lungs. It's fine. Jay gets it."

"My point is, you have a huge heart, Jaybird. And you're one of the most generous people in this town. Your family isn't just Proud because that's your name. They're proud for real because you make them that way every single day."

Tucker nodded. "Last week, your cousin Ginny-Rae was bragging about how you looked after her two older kids so she could bring Baby Rae for her checkup."

Dunn poked a blunt fingertip on the wooden table. "And let's not forget the time back in high school when you helped Gracie out after she got into her first car accident. My parents still talk about you like you were God's gift to stranded teenagers, even though you'd barely gotten your license yourself."

Dunn's sister had been sobbing and gasping from fear even though she'd only sideswiped one of those orange barrels out on the Nuthatch Road. "That wasn't a big deal, but thank you for saying it."

I did feel a little better after their kind words, and now that Dunn had pointed it out, I realized he was a dairy farmer hooked up with a fancy doctor. It was obvious Tucker thought the world of Dunn and had no problem with Dunn's work or his country manners.

"Ask Lane out," Tucker advised softly. "Really. Because I can tell you from personal experience that just because he has a bunch of fancy degrees, that doesn't make him less of a fool when it comes to his heart."

My stomach twisted with nerves at the idea of trying to ask Lane for something formal—like *dating* instead of fucking. He was too nice to laugh in my face, but I would die if I saw him scramble to come up with a polite excuse as to why that wasn't a good idea.

When Cassandra at the counter called my name, I jumped. "Okay, well," I said, pushing to stand. "I appreciate the pep talk. I'll be thinking about it."

Probably all night long.

And more than likely, I wouldn't get up the nerve to act on it for a while.

I patted Tucker on the shoulder as I walked past to go to the cashier for my order. Ten minutes later, I was home with a giant brown paper bag full of delicious-smelling food. I scribbled a quick note inviting Lane to dinner at my house and stuck it on his door before heading out back to check on the guys.

Disco Dave spread his tail feathers as soon as he saw me and squawked to get my attention. I went through the necessary chores to care for them before bidding them a good night and retreating to the workroom in the garage where my Entwinin' work had taken over most of the space.

I'd gone back and forth for weeks about the idea of making Lane an Entwinin' wreath, but every time, I'd managed to talk myself out of it. I'd never made a wreath for someone I was interested in before, and if I did it for Lane, it would be a big deal. Everyone in town would know how I felt about him... and if Lane didn't realize the significance for himself, someone in town would probably point it out.

But maybe that was a good thing. Maybe by April, I'd be ready to put my feelings on the line.

Despite all my misgivings, I *had* put aside a quantity of thin, whippy wisteria vines—the hardest to get since they were the best kind for twinin'—from my stock at the beginning of the season, like deep down, I'd known the wreath, like my growing feelings for Lane, was inevitable.

So I sat down at my table in the cold garage and got to work on the idea I had for a Georgia Bulldog. The University of Georgia was an important part of Lane's life. Georgia fans were rabid anyway, but he'd spent a huge part of his life there. I sketched out a base and added a few more components, as well—the things I liked best about Lane, the things that made me think of him. There were a surprising number for the short time I'd known the man.

I got so excited about the project I tuned out the rest of the world... at least until I heard Lane's car rumbling down the driveway an hour later. Then I jumped up, put away my sketches, and headed out to give the handsome man his nightly *"Howdy, neighbor"* to collect his sweet, stammering hello in return and to lose myself in the warmth of his presence.

Because while I wasn't educated, I was smart enough to enjoy a good thing when I had it.

And Lane Desmond was maybe the best thing that had ever happened to me.

Chapter Five

Lane

By the end of February, the Entwinin' festival seemed to be all anyone was talking about.

"I'm just saying, we have extra wisteria vines in the back if you need any," Hunter said as he leaned over his kitchen island to set a cup of coffee by my elbow. I'd stopped by to take a look at his pet turkey poult, Tammy Wynette, who seemed to be thriving if a little spoiled, and when he'd offered me a drink, I'd taken the chance to get out of the blustery gray day.

The truth was, Hunter and Charlie's kitchen had become one of my favorite places in the Thicket. It was always bright and cheerful, always smelled like Thanksgiving—probably because the men stocked up enough food at the Thicket's side-dish festival, the Gobblin', to last all year—and always made my chest feel warm and tight in a good way. Charlie and Hunter gave each other shit constantly, but the love they had for each other was audible in every teasing word.

I finished making a note about when Tammy might

need her next vaccine before giving Hunter a curious look. "That's nice of you, but what would *I* need wisteria for?"

"Well, because... uh." Hunter looked flummoxed for a moment before casually hip-checking the man beside him. "Tell him, Charlie."

"Because of the Entwinin', of course." Charlie looked up from where he'd been peeling the skin off a few cloves of garlic. "Oh, shit, Lane. I bet no one's told you about—"

"They have," I assured him. "Hunter mentioned it months ago, and Jay works on wreaths every night before we —" I cleared my throat, feeling my cheeks go hot. "That is to say, I've noticed that Jaybird makes wreaths. But the festival's not until early April, right?"

"True." Charlie rested his hands on the counter and leaned across, making eye contact with me. "But the Entwinin's not a last-minute sort of thing. Not if you do it right. Anyone who wants to make a good wreath needs to source their vines now before the only ones left are the old, dried-up, gnarly ones. You want to make a good wreath, don't you?"

I looked between the two of them. "Why would I make a wreath at all? They're mostly for couples, aren't they? Or best friends?"

Hunter and Charlie exchanged one of their looks that was more like a whole conversation, the shorthand of partners who knew and loved each other well. I took a sip of coffee while I contemplated what they weren't saying.

Charlie raised one eyebrow and tilted his head toward me.

Hunter shook his head—a single, insistent negative.

Charlie raised a second eyebrow.

Hunter set his jaw.

Charlie bit his lip, and his gaze went liquid and pleading.

Hunter's shoulders slumped, and he sighed.

"That's... mostly true, Lane," Hunter said carefully. "Entwinin' wreaths aren't like Valentine's cards, where you give them to just anyone. Or like Christmas wreaths, where you put one on the door to celebrate the season in general. A wreath is a gesture of affection for the most important person or people in your life. A way of saying you love and appreciate them."

I nodded. I knew this.

"And do you... I mean... can you think of anyone you'd like to give a wreath to?" he prompted. "Maybe... someone you spend all your free time with, and talk about constantly, and who smiles at you so hard he once walked into a street sign in broad daylight, just as an example?"

Jay's handsome face and sweet, goofy smile swam through my mind, and as usual, just thinking about the man made me sigh happily.

A few weeks ago, I'd thought we were total opposites—like a fish and a bird—but now I knew better. We were different, sure, but in the way that bees and flowers were different. Somehow, our differences worked.

We weren't sweethearts, though.

Nope.

We were *friends*... though I wouldn't flatter myself that I was Jay's best friend since he had many.

We were... friends with benefits.

Casual friends with benefits.

The kind who ate dinner together most nights before the benefits began, then shared a bed after the benefits were over, and had established sides of the bed... for benefit reasons only.

Friends who did thoughtful, casual things, like bringing each other snacks every single day at a specific time and taking care of a small muster of peacocks together every morning.

Friends who spent all their free time together because, at least in my case, there was no one in the world I'd rather spend time with, and everything felt right and easy when I was with him, and...

I sucked in a breath.

Oh my God, Jaybird Proud was my sweetheart.

How the hell had that happened?

My mind immediately tried to reject the idea. If my last relationship had taught me anything, it was that I didn't know shit about relationships. I didn't know how to be emotionally available. I didn't know how to do romance. It had taken Chad just a couple of weeks after our breakup to find himself someone better. It was only a matter of time until Jay figured this out.

But at the same time... now that I'd acknowledged them to myself, I found I couldn't deny my feelings for Jay.

My *Entwinin'* feelings.

I wanted Jay to know how amazing and special he was...

But how could I tell him without, you know, *telling* him?

"Lane?" Charlie waved a hand in front of my face. "Hey, Lane?"

"Huh?" I glanced up blankly.

"Great." Charlie lifted his hands and let them flop at his sides. "We broke him."

"We? This conversation was your idea," Hunter pointed out.

Charlie lifted his chin. "You're my fiancé. My ideas are *our* ideas."

Hunter laughed and tugged on Charlie's hair. "Sure they are, baby. I'll remember this when *I* have an idea tonight. Hey, Lane? Is everything alright?"

"Yeah. No, yeah, I'm great. I just, uh..." My cheeks burned. "Do people ever make Entwinin' wreaths in secret? Like from a secret admirer?" I asked, trying to be vague and generalized.

Hunter pierced me with a look. "If you're making a wreath for Jaybird Proud, you'd better give it to him in person."

"Jay? Who said anything about... Why would I make a wreath for Jay? Don't be ridiculous."

Hunter and Charlie exchanged a look before Charlie set down his garlic press, moved around the island, and perched on the stool next to me. "You probably don't know this, but when you talk about Jay, the tips of your ears turn red, and your eyelashes do a strange, fluttery thing."

Hunter snorted, and Charlie muttered an affectionate curse at him before focusing back on me. "It's actually very sweet. I can't think of a more deserving person than Jaybird Proud, nor can I think of a kinder man to set you up with."

"W-we're not *dating*," I stammered, concentrating on keeping my eyelashes still. "Exactly."

"Fine," Charlie said with an eye roll. "But consider making him a wreath anyway."

Hunter added, "Jay's made hundreds of wreaths for others over the years, but I'm not sure he's actually ever received one."

My eyes snapped over to his. "Never?"

I remembered Jay saying he'd never made a wreath for a sweetheart, but it seemed unbelievable that no one had ever made one for him. Jay was the most generous man in town.

The kindest man I'd ever met. He was beautiful inside and out.

"So he's never had a... like a..." I tried to say the word *boyfriend*, but the very idea of him dating someone made the coffee in my stomach turn sour.

"No," Hunter said with a knowing grin. "At least, not that I know of or that the town's known of. Not for lack of setups, though. He's a prime target for the town matchmakers, poor guy."

Charlie looked at Hunter. "Did the two of you ever...?"

My stomach dropped when Hunter bounced his eyebrows back at Charlie. "Bow chicka bow wow," he sang, rotating his hips. "Where to begin with me and Jay? Let's see..." He put his fingertip on his chin and pursed his lips.

I tried to imagine that finger or those lips on Jay—*my* Jay —and the idea made me sick.

"You're upsetting Lane," Charlie warned with a growl.

"Ah, it's *Lane* who's upset. Riiiight." Hunter turned to wink at me. "No, Jay and I never did anything. Correction, we went out for a beer one time, but we ended up mediating a fight between Hux and Kev. I believe it was in regards to pilfered apples, although they seemed to be magical, video game apples... which was a bit confusing and required quite a bit of detailed explanation. Before I knew it, I was knee-deep in harvesting pixelated virility gourds." He shuddered. "I ended up having to do a six-week detox course just to stop caring about my homestead and orchards."

Charlie muttered, "Don't get him started talking about *Horn of Glory*, or poor Tammy Wynette will die of old age before you get a chance to give her a follow-up visit."

Hunter shot him a look. "I'm clean. One thousand days *HOG* sober. And don't worry. Jay didn't take to the video game like I did."

"So you never hooked up with Jay?" I asked, just for clarification's sake.

"No. Never." He tilted his head. "Have *you?*"

I let out a breath. "Yes. We... we're hooking up."

"You don't say," Charlie said in a dry voice.

"And... and I think I want it to be more than that," I went on in a whisper. The realization made my heart beat like hummingbird wings. "It's just... I suck at relationships. After my last breakup, I swore I was never going to do that again. At least, not anytime soon. And here I am, wanting more with Jay..."

"Jay's a good man," Hunter said. "One of the best."

"I know. He's always there to lend a hand. And the man would rather die than ever let you pay him back. He's... he's amazing. But that doesn't mean I know how to be a good boyfriend."

Charlie slid an arm around Hunter's waist and leaned against his side. "Actually, Lane... you'd be surprised. Finding the right guy sometimes makes all the difference."

Hunter pressed a kiss to Charlie's head. "Agreed. Relationships require two people caring enough to make them work. When they end, it's never just one person's fault."

I took a breath and considered this. When Chad had blamed me, I'd believed him because he was right—I *hadn't* been as invested in our relationship as I should have been. But I couldn't imagine not caring about Jay's happiness. The man had fascinated me from the beginning, even when I'd been mistrusting and befuddled by his kindness.

"But... what if I tell Jay I want more, and it doesn't work out? Everyone in town will know. It'll be awkward as fuck."

Charlie nodded. "The small-town thing's hard to get used to."

"Actually, it's the opposite. Athens is a small place, too.

Everyone knew everything about Chad and me, which was why I wanted to move away after our breakup and his marriage. I want to be with Jay, but I don't want everyone else's business in my business about it."

Charlie shook his head. "That's not really an option here, I'm afraid. Less than forty-eight hours after Hunter and I went official, people started getting involved. Someone—my money's on Hunter's sister—anonymously dropped off a congratulatory lube basket... which is exactly what it sounds like, by the way."

A snicker burbled out of me, and I clapped my hand over my mouth.

"At least the lube was useful and, like you said, *anonymous*." Hunter's tone was aggrieved. "Unlike your grandfather cornering me outside the Tavern to discuss 'a Nutter man's unique needs' and make sure I'd be 'a good provider.' Don't you dare laugh, Charlton. I was afraid he'd offer me a demonstration."

Laughing, Charlie buried his face in Hunter's chest. "I know, baby. I know. It was awful... but also kinda sweet. Meddling comes with the territory around here, I'm afraid."

I groaned. "So you're telling me I need to bite the bullet? Just... wreath him in front of the whole town and tell him flat out that I've developed real feelings for him? We haven't even been on a date."

Hunter shrugged. "You could always tell him with tots first. It's the time-honored tradition here, after all."

I glanced back and forth between them, wondering what the fuck they were talking about. "Tots? As in... children?"

"Nope. As in taters. Shredded potatoes." Hunter settled himself on a stool while Charlie went back to pressing garlic into the giant pot of spaghetti sauce he was making. Hunter's voice was no longer teasing, and I could tell he wanted to help. "See, we have a date restaurant here," he began. "You might say it's the romance capital of the Thicket. And if you take your honey to the Steak n' Bait—"

"No." I glanced between them. "The Steak n' Bait? Come on."

"You live in a town that celebrates the Lickin', the Bobbin', the Gobblin', and the Entwinin', Lane." Charlie tapped the side of his spoon against his pot of sauce. "Of course it's called the Steak n' Bait."

Well, when he put it like that...

"At the Steak n' Bait," Hunter continued, "they serve a famous dish of tater tots all done up with toppings. It's to die for. But back in the day, before they got their auto-shredder, it took a while for them to make 'em. It became a tradition that you'd only order tots when you were with someone you didn't mind spending all that time with." He grinned. "Folks started saying stuff like, 'Now, *that's* a guy I wouldn't mind waitin' on tots with.'"

Charlie nodded. "It kinda took on a life of its own, like most things in the Thicket do, and became a symbol of love and commitment. It means you're on an important date... or you're proposing marriage."

"Tater tots?" I asked, just to be sure. "Are a symbol of love and commitment?"

He nodded slowly. "You can't explain small-town traditions, Lane. You just have to live them."

"I... see."

"Jaybird Proud is an integral part of this town," Hunter pointed out. "He's lived here his whole life, and he speaks in the language of the Thicket. If you want to confess heartfelt feelings in a way he'll really understand... do it with tots and twinin'."

After finishing our conversation and another cup of coffee, I headed home.

On the short drive to the house, I was so full of affection for Jay, so happy with my decision to confess my feelings to him, I decided to do both.

I'd make reservations for lunch at the Steak n' Bait, *and* I'd make him his very own Entwinin' wreath to give to him at the festival.

If Licking Thicket was part of who Jay was—and I could see that plain as day—then I would make sure Jay knew I saw that part of him and loved it too.

When I parked and got out of my car, I took a deep breath of bracing winter air and let it out. This was the right decision, and I didn't want to fuck it up. I would take my time about it and get it right... and figure out how the hell one twined a wreath in the first place.

In the meantime, I would spend as much time enjoying Jay as he'd let me.

Granted, our work schedules were busy. I was working extra hours since springtime's babies had already begun arriving on the local farms, and Jay was working tons washing winter-crusted cars and preparing for the Entwinin' festival.

But we'd find time. Starting right now.

Jay's truck was in the drive which meant he was around here somewhere. Since Kasey Musgraves was crooning in the garage, I decided to check his workroom first.

No luck.

"Jay?" I called.

"Back here!" His voice came from the storage closet in the back where he'd meticulously organized shelves with open bins on them, holding all kinds of various sizes and lengths of wisteria vines.

I found him in the closet with his shirt off, and my brain immediately turned to squishy, half-baked dough. "*Ngh.*"

He turned and grinned, one slightly crooked tooth pressing his lip out in a sexy way that drew my attention and made me want him even more. "Hey, sexy," he said.

"Diggin' the no-shirt look," I managed to grunt.

His eyes heated. "Diggin' that look in your eyes."

I moved closer until my body pressed his against the shelves. Thank God they were sturdy. My hands immediately went to his rounded pecs and squeezed. "Let me suck you off."

"*Let* you?" he asked with a teasing glint in his eye. "That's an interesting choice of words, Dr. Desmond. Why should I let you have your wicked way with my person?"

I moved my hands down to unfasten his jeans. There was no way on earth his answer would be no, and we both knew it.

"Let's see," I began as I shoved his jeans and underwear down. "I'm very dedicated. Talented, some might say. I'm also eager to please."

I moved in and began pressing kisses down his chest, tasting a combination of salt and sawdust that was uniquely Jay.

"I'm well-versed in anatomy," I continued, dragging my tongue down his Adonis belt and into the thatch of hair above the root of his hard cock. "I'm... I'm..." His heavy balls and warm cock drew my attention, and I leaned in to rub my face against them.

"Distractable?" he teased, tangling his fingers in my hair.

I licked and sucked, enjoying his hitched breaths and deep rumbles of satisfaction and appreciation.

"You sure are eager to make an impression," he gasped when I took his cock as deep into my throat as I could and subsequently gagged on it.

"Fuck my mouth," I muttered, reaching around to grab his ass.

"Jesus fuck, Lane." He thrust into my throat and tightened his grip on my hair. "Not gonna last. So fucking good."

My own cock ached, so I reached down to open my pants and stroke it. Sucking Jay off turned me on. Imagining what we looked like in the dimly lit closet with me on my knees and him thrusting hard into my throat made my orgasm come barreling on.

I choked on his cock, stroking us both quickly and irregularly. Jay's hand cupped the back of my head as he guided me. "That's it, baby. You're doing so good. Gonna make me come."

My release hit seconds before his did. His hot spunk landed on my face as I pulled back with a gasp and sucked in a breath. The sounds of our groaning, the scent of his cum, and the possessive feel of his hands on me were all fucking amazing.

"Lane, what the fuck?" he murmured as he tried catching his breath. "Get up here. C'mere."

I stood awkwardly and tried tucking myself back in, but Jay shoved my hands away and cupped my face instead to meet my eyes. "That was fucking amazing. Thank you."

I preened at the praise, feeling my chest puff out a little. I'd wanted to please him, wanted to impress him with my skills and my strong attraction to him.

Most of all, I wanted to make him happy.

I leaned in and kissed him long and hard before pulling back. "I'm in the mood for spaghetti. What do you think?"

Jay's face widened into a grin. "Do you one better. I made Italian Gentleman. It's in the oven already."

My chest filled with fluttery strangeness. If this man wasn't careful, I was going to want to tie myself to him with something way stronger than wisteria vines.

Chapter Six

Jay

Through the month of March, I took every opportunity to touch and kiss and suck Lane Desmond. To care for him and pretend he was mine.

I wasn't fooling myself into thinking he actually *was* mine. Not really. There were about a billion reasons why he wasn't and could never be—as many reasons as there were degrees on his walls and vocabulary words he knew that I didn't, and those things *mattered*, even if Dunn and Tucker said otherwise—but I sure enjoyed pretending.

I rolled out of my bed quietly, one hand on the bed frame to keep it from creaking under my weight. Spring was arriving in the Thicket slowly but surely, which made getting out of bed in the morning a little bit easier... not that you'd know it to look at Lane.

The second I left the bed, he rolled into my warm spot and immediately pulled the covers around him, half his face buried in my pillow and the other half catching the pale morning light. The poor man's hair stuck up in every direction, like he'd been fighting a hard battle... and I supposed he had since it was the start of calving season, and Alva had called him for an assist at Dunn Johnson's place last night.

I leaned against my doorjamb for a second and watched him sleep like the creepiest creeper to ever creep. The man needed his rest, and I didn't want to wake him... but *dang*, I really liked looking at Lane.

Even a couple of months ago, he'd carried himself like he was holding something back. For a man who always knew what to do when it came to animals, Lane had been nervous as a jackrabbit around the people of the Thicket. More and more these days, though—in these quiet moments when he was tangled up in my blankets, or when we sat on my couch drinking a beer, or even sometimes when he was out and about in town, chatting with Cindy Ann Johnson and some of the other ladies about Thicket happenings—he looked calmer.

More peaceful.

Happier, maybe.

God, I really, really hoped he was happy in the Thicket... and with me.

I shook my head at myself. "Don't get used to it, Jay," I muttered under my breath. "It's not forever."

Lane had made it clear that he wanted casual—light and easy, with no strings—and I was fine with that.

I *was*.

Completely fine.

Except... *fuck*, I really wasn't.

The truth was, I had this stupid hope buried deep in my chest that one day Lane might be okay with getting un-casual. One might even say... serious. In short, I'd like to Entwine the hell out of the man.

I wanted more mornings like this, where Lane was

sweet and sleepy in my bed, and more nights where the two of us laughed and teased and solved the world's problems over Italian Gentleman. I wanted, really badly, for him to stop seeing me as a guy he was killing time with. But I wasn't sure what to do about it other than what I *had* been doing—floating along, falling in love, and pretending I wasn't.

I knew a whole fuckton about how to give *other* people what they wanted and needed, whether it was Mrs. Holcombe needing her groceries carried when her twins started throwing surround-sound temper tantrums in the middle of the grocery store or my grandma Emmaline needing a "wearable" Entwinin' plaque for her husband Amos to commemorate him winning Best Mature Bovine Herder at the Lickin' last summer.

But wanting Lane for myself was a whole other thing. It felt selfish and scary. It tied me up in knots... and not the pretty Entwinin' kind.

The truth was, I'd just never found anything worth wanting before. Not the way I wanted him.

"Jay?" Lane opened one eye and blinked at me blearily. "Y'okay?"

My stomach tightened. I wanted to say, "Yeah, Lane. As long as you're here with me, I'm very okay." But that wouldn't be casual, would it? I didn't want to put pressure on the man. I definitely didn't want to see him do his jackrabbit impression again.

"Oh, yeah. Sorry. Just got distracted thinking of my to-do list today. The Entwinin' is tomorrow, and I've got like five wreaths I need to finish up. But first, breakfast for Dave and the gang... and then for my favorite veterinarian."

Lane's eye slid closed, but his face creased in a sleepy grin. "Always helping. S'cute."

I snorted as I threw on a sweatshirt and let myself out to the backyard, where my flock of cocks strolled around their enclosure. Just as Lane had predicted, Disco Dave had laid off the peacock Viagra once he'd settled into his new enclosure, complete with roosts and lots of soft pine shavings. He still shook out his feathers, of course, but not in the aggressive, train-rattling way he'd done at first.

"Dave's figured out that his mating season will come eventually, and he's gotta be patient," Lane had said when he'd looked over the flock a few weeks back. "Speaking of which, I have this friend back in Georgia who happens to have some peahens…"

My smile had taken up my whole face. The words Lane spoke could've come out of my own mouth. I couldn't resist teasing him. "Seems like a lot of your stories start that way these days, Doc."

Lane had blushed a mouthwatering pink from his head to his collarbone. "Yes. Well. Possibly. In any case, about the peahens…"

Lane liked to joke about my obsession with taking care of people and putting other people's wants before my own, but Lane worried about the animals in his care like they were his own family. He didn't just do his job; he *lived* it, pouring his heart into every furry or feathered creature that crossed his path. He was thoughtful and honest, always saying exactly what he meant, even when it wasn't what I wanted to hear. He made people—*me*—feel like we mattered. And he was so damn appreciative of even the littlest kindness.

It was no wonder I'd fallen for him hard and just kept falling.

Once again, I was not an idiot.

I wished the peacocks a good day, then went back inside

and washed up. Preparing breakfast for Lane was second nature by now since I got the privilege of doing it three or four days a week. I whipped up some scrambled eggs, bacon, and toast. Without thinking about it, I grabbed the honey jar out of the pantry and set it on my kitchen island.

The first few times I'd stayed at Lane's place, I'd noticed him drizzling honey on his toast, so I'd bought some at the farmer's market. Now, whenever he reached for it automatically, like he was used to it always being there, it gave me a little thrill.

I shook my head at myself. One of these days, the man was going to figure out that I never ate the stuff myself. He was going to recognize that this honey was a gesture of... of... un-casualness... and I was going to feel like a fool.

Still, I couldn't see to stop myself.

A few minutes later, Lane's footsteps shuffled across the floor.

"You know you're ridiculous, right?" Lane's voice was warm and scratchy, still thick with sleep.

I glanced over my shoulder, nearly dropping my bacon spatula. Lane's hair was wilder than I'd ever seen it, and he had a deep crease down his cheek. He'd grabbed a long-sleeved Bovines Alumni T-shirt from my drawer, and seeing it on him was making me, uh... *display*... in a way that Dave would be mightily jealous of.

"Am I?" I said, forcing myself to look closely at the eggs so Lane wouldn't see whatever foolish look was on my face.

"Mmm." He flopped onto one of the kitchen stools. "Barely dawn and you're playing short-order cook. And I happen to know you were in your workshop past midnight."

He knew because that was where he'd found me when he'd come home, himself.

I chuckled. "Gotta make sure folks have a happy

Entwinin'. Liz Stoke has been waiting a whole year to propose to Crystal Rivera 'cause she wanted to do it with a wreath. An Entwinin' wreath is the purest form of love there is."

"Sure," he agreed, but when I turned toward him to plate the eggs, I noticed a little frown on Lane's forehead.

"You okay?" I asked, setting his plate in front of him.

Lane reached for the honey and paused for a second before he started drizzling honey on his bread. When he looked up at me, his eyes were soft. "Yeah. I'm great. Thank you for breakfast."

"No big deal." I turned back to the counter and gave it a wipe, even though it didn't need it.

The sound of Lane's crunching toast filled the quiet, and I glanced over to watch him chew with his eyes half-closed like it was the best thing he'd eaten in days.

I couldn't help but smile to myself.

"So, um..." Lane finished eating and set his fork down a little nervously. "I've got a short day at the clinic today. Want to meet me for lunch? Say... noon?"

I blinked, caught off guard. We'd never done lunch before. Breakfast, sure. Dinners too, mostly at home. Lunch felt... different. It was the time of day when all the Thicket gossips would be out and about. Not that I expected Lane to, like, lay one on me in the middle of the Thicket Tavern or anything.

Though I sure wouldn't mind if he did.

Could this be a step toward un-casual? Or is it just lunch?

Suddenly, I felt nervous too, and my mind flew downstairs to the best, most important Entwinin' wreath I'd ever made—one I'd started designing back in February 'cause it needed to be special, a wreath to end all wreaths—and would probably never have the guts to give the man I wanted to be Entwined with.

"Yeah," I managed to choke out. "Yeah, I could do lunch. I'll meet you at the clinic."

By the time I walked into the clinic at 11:59, I'd ridden a roller coaster up and down ten times, alternately hoping this lunch was a sign of un-casual-ness and convinced this was a prelude to a breakup... or whatever you called it when you weren't actually together.

When I opened the door, the bell above it jingled. Lane had been in the middle of talking—"Pete, can you update Jinx's file to say—" but he came to a halt as he caught sight of me and smiled sweetly.

The roller coaster went up again, sending a warmth through my chest I didn't know what to do with.

"Howdy, neighbor," I managed.

It looked like Lane was trying to restrain his grin, maybe to be professional or something, but he couldn't quite do it. "Hey."

"Dear God," Petey groaned. "This is like the anal glands all over again. You're late, Jay," he informed me. "It's nearly noon. Snack time's come and gone."

I blinked at him. "Everything okay, Petey?"

He sighed. "Actually? No. No, it's not. I've been on thirty-two dates in the past two months, and none of them have gone anywhere for... well, reasons... and now I'm out of options." His cheeks blushed. "And meanwhile, I've had to watch a couple of guys who are a hundred percent head over heels for each other wring their hands and dance around each other, utterly oblivious."

"Ooof." I shook my head. "That's rough. Some people, huh?"

Petey inhaled a sharp breath through his nose. "Yeah,

Jay. Some people." He shook his head. "And it's *Pete* now. Or Peter. Petey makes me sound like a freckled nine-year-old."

I looked Petey—er, *Pete*—over, taking in his short stature, messy hair, and the line of tiny brown spots over the bridge of his nose. I opened my mouth to say something... but when I saw the look in his eyes, I realized immediately that it would be better unsaid.

"Right," I said instead. "*Pete*. Got it."

Pete lifted one eyebrow in Lane's direction. "So what's the occasion for lunch today? Pre-gaming the Entwinin'? Gonna talk about, you know... wreaths? Love declarations? Stuff like that?"

Lane's face went red, and he stared at the wall. "N-no—"

"Jay..." Pete cocked his head at me. "You have lots of experience in the Entwinin' game. You're practically the Thicket's Entwinin' expert. Anything *you're* particularly looking forward to tomorrow?"

"I, uh... Well, I..." I glanced at my feet.

Before I could come up with an answer, the bell over the door jangled again. I was too busy trying to get my hot cheeks to cool off to see who'd arrived, but when Pete did, he inhaled sharply.

"Oh my God. My dry spell may be over," he whispered under his breath. Then he summoned a blinding smile and said more loudly, "Good afternoon! May I help you?"

"Lane!" the newcomer said, his voice smooth, confident... and entirely too loud for the clinic's front room.

Lane turned his head as if he'd heard a ghost. "Chad?"

I stepped aside as the newcomer strode toward the desk. He was tall and broad-shouldered, wearing a suit sharp enough to cut glass. His hair was perfect, his watch glittered under the fluorescent lights, and his smile was polished and practiced. *Smarmy*, I thought immediately... which was an unkind thought, yes, but that didn't make it untrue.

It became even more true when the man pulled Lane into a quick embrace, complete with a kiss on his cheek like something out of a movie.

Pete's jaw dropped. "Who is *this*?" he whispered to me, but I hadn't the first clue.

Lane extracted himself from the hug. "Pete. Jay. This is... this is Chad. My ex-boyfriend."

This? *This* was Lane's ex? I wasn't quite sure how I felt about that, but the thought occurred to me that if I found the man's car in a ditch, I wouldn't offer him a tow.

Not for free, anyway.

Pete immediately stepped out from behind the desk, inserting himself between Chad and Lane. "Hey. Peter Winchell: vet tech, supply wizard, *currently single*. Lovely to meet you, Chad."

Chad's eyes flicked over Pete with polite interest. "Likewise, I'm sure."

"Chad..." Behind Pete, Lane shook his head. "What are you doing here?" I liked to think he didn't sound overjoyed to see the man.

"I was in the area meeting with an old colleague, and I thought I'd stop by and take you to lunch. We have a lot of catching up to do. I heard you'd ended up practicing in a small town but hadn't quite believed it." His gaze swept around the front room and then out onto the street, where a couple of people were canoodling under a wisteria bower. "It's... something, isn't it?"

Though his smile didn't slip even a fraction, I could tell he didn't think that "something" was anything good.

Lane gave me a helpless look I couldn't interpret, and

then his jaw firmed. "Actually, Chad, I already have lunch plans..."

Suddenly, I thought I understood Lane's look. He wanted me to bow out gracefully so I wouldn't make him uncomfortable. "Oh! No, Lane. Don't, uh, don't worry about me." I put both hands up. "You two can go ahead. I'll catch up with you later. At home."

"Home?" Chad asked curiously, his eyes ping-ponging from Lane to me and back again.

Lane blushed. "Yes. I mean..." His face turned a red so deep it looked painful. "Jay and I... Jay is my..."

He gave me another helpless look, but this time, I caught on faster. "Landlord," I supplied. "Yep. I'm Jaybird Proud, and I lord Lane's land. As his landlord."

Pete, Chad, and Lane gave me identical slack-jawed looks. Lane was the first to recover. "Jay is my friend," he said firmly, "and the best man I know. He and I have lunch plans at the Steak n' Bait."

I had to suck in a breath, partly because the way Lane defended me made my chest squeeze and partly because the Steak n' Bait... well, I wasn't sure anyone had ever explained it to Lane, but that restaurant had a particular reputation. It was the Thicket's number one spot for romance, at least according to the Yelp reviews, and so many proposals had taken place there they kept a running tally on the big sign out front, even though Chuck Gimbal had to climb a ladder once a week to update it.

Unfortunately, Lane ruined the effect of all this after a long moment of awkward silence by telling Chad with grudging politeness, "But you can come with us, if you'd like... I guess?"

Chad smiled like Lane had sent him an engraved invitation. "Perfect!" He gave me a look that made me wish I'd changed my boots for something that didn't probably have peacock poop stuck to the bottom and that I'd worn a shirt with sleeves. "We can take my Lexus."

Unfortunately, things only went downhill from there.

Riding in the back seat of Chad's Lexus was a special kind of hell—one where I worried what kind of stains my boots were leaving on his pristine cream interior while Chad updated Lane on the lives of every single friend they'd ever had in common—and it didn't improve once we got to the Steak n' Bait (currently boasting 2,726 YESSES AND COUNTING).

"Doc Lane!" Barbara McNamara gushed the second we opened the door. "How are you? You know, everyone wants our dinner special, but hardly anyone takes advantage of our lunch offerings, and we were all just so tickled when you called to make a reservation for you and... and..." Her eyes took in Chad's tall form standing between us, and she pressed her lips together. "Oh." She blinked. "There may have been a mix-up."

"Story of my life," Lane muttered. More loudly, he said, "There'll be three of us for lunch now."

I'd say he blushed, except he hadn't *stopped* blushing since the moment Chad arrived... which sorta told me everything I needed to know about how Lane felt about Chad, didn't it? Still, Lane had invited me. Lane had insisted. So... for Lane, I'd stick around.

The place was fairly quiet at lunchtime—ladies in nice dresses chatted over cocktails while folks in business suits brokered billion-dollar deals... or whatever corporate types did at lunch. Barbara guided us past them to a two-person table way in the back that had been set with flowers. She paused awkwardly.

"Uh. Maybe... maybe this one instead." Barbara spun

toward a four-person table and placed our menus down. "I'll just... um..." She twisted her hands. "I'll go see where your server is."

Chad took a seat, and Jay and I followed.

"This place is cute," Chad decided. "Lane, you remember the time you and me and Mark Levy went out for dinner to that nouveau cuisine restaurant with the fake fireplace?"

"I remember getting food poisoning," Lane said tightly. "And riding home in the Uber alone."

"Oh." Chad frowned. "God, I forgot that part."

For the first time in my life, I had the urge to commit murder... or, at the very least, to hit a man directly in the face.

How the hell had Lane been with someone so *mean*? I thought maybe I understood now why he reacted to the smallest kindness like a plant in the desert after a nice cool rain.

It was like a gift from the heavens when Kelsey came bustling over with a huge tray, interrupting Chad's reminiscing.

"Happy Entwinin', you two!" Kelsey smiled broadly as she set down a plate in the center of the table... and only then seemed to do a quick head count. "Um. *Three?*" She frowned like she was recounting.

I frowned, too, when I saw what she'd placed on the table. "These are tots, Kels."

"Well, yeah. I know." She shifted her weight from foot to foot. "On account of... Barbara said she offered Lane the pre-Entwinin' lunch special when he called to make the reservation."

Ah, shit. I immediately realized what must've happened. Lane had been trying to do a nice thing, inviting me to lunch, and he'd accepted Barbara's offer in all innocence. But the man didn't understand why tater tots were significant in the Thicket in the same way that he didn't understand that the Steak n' Bait wasn't just a normal lunch spot.

Around here, sharing a plate of tots wasn't just about enjoying a crunchy shredded potato; it was a declaration. The equivalent of a promise ring. One step up from being in a relationship, one half step down from happily-ever-after-let's-adopt-some-pets.

A man didn't casually partake of tots with a hookup.

He sure as hell didn't partake of them with an ex.

Tots were the opposite of casual.

For a second, I debated whether I could simply let it go. Lane didn't realize what he'd be doing if he ate tots with both of us, and neither did Chad. But I'd been born and raised in this town. I was Thicket to the bone, and I'd be damned if I let Lane—*my* Lane—eat tots with another man while I sat by.

"Take them away," I told Kelsey. To Lane, I added, "Been overdoing it on the fried foods. I'd sooner stick to salad, to start."

Lane's blush intensified for some reason, but he nodded unhappily. "Right. Salad appetizers for everyone," he told Kelsey. "Good idea."

"So, Jay," Chad said sometime later after Kelsey had left with the offending tots. "Tell me about yourself. You're Lane's landlord?"

"Yep." I set my elbows on the table, then vaguely remembered that was supposed to be bad manners and scooted them off again. "He lives over my workroom." Lane looked like he might be feeling uncomfortable, so I added, "Best tenant I ever had. I hope he'll stay forever."

Lane glanced at me, and one side of his mouth ticked up in a smile.

"Uh-huh. And where do you work?" Chad made it sound like an idle question, but I knew it wasn't.

"I do lots of things. For example, I recently started a small peacock-rental enterprise. Thinking of calling it Jay Proud's Peacocks, but I'm still workshopping it. Primarily, though, you'll find me at the Suds Barn, the Thicket's best and only car wash."

"You... wash cars," Chad said like this wasn't obvious. "For a living."

"Sure do." I grinned. "Most satisfying job in the world, getting to fix things up and make 'em shine."

"Jay's excellent at what he does. He's also an artist." Lane gave me an encouraging smile. "He carves things out of wood, and he twines the most beautiful wreaths for our Entwinin' festival—"

Chad blinked. "Your... what?"

"The Entwinin'." Lane gave Chad a look. "It's like Valentine's Day, but instead of cheap candy hearts, you celebrate by twining wisteria vines into a special shape for your loved one. It's very sentimental."

"If you say so."

"It *is*," Lane insisted. "People work hard on their wreaths for months, Chad. It's a sign of commitment to a relationship. It's a sign of emotional vulnerability. It's a sign of... of love."

Wow. I hadn't realized that Lane had become such a fan of the Entwinin', but he'd nailed it.

Chad blinked, then glanced back and forth between me and Lane. His eyebrows winged up. "Are you serious?" he demanded. "Lane, come on..."

"Lane's right," I cut in because I didn't understand what

had put that incredulous look on Chad's face, but I decided I didn't like it. "It might sound silly to an outsider, but... lots of romantic things do, when you think about it. Who decided the only way to love someone was with hearts and... and... diapered babies with wings? Cupid just had a good PR person. What matters is the love you put into a thing. What matters is taking the time to do something special for the person you care about and making them feel seen and appreciated and wanted and... and important."

I broke off, feeling my own cheeks go hot. I was just talking about my own feelings for Lane now, and from the look on Chad's face, he knew it.

Lane gave me a tremulous little smile, though, so I figured I hadn't embarrassed myself too much.

Chad, on the other hand, frowned. "Huhhhh."

I could hear the sound of Lane's teeth grinding together from across the table. "Chad," he snapped. "Why are you actually here? And don't give me lies about being in the neighborhood. Is Simon..."

"Simon's great." Chad's thumb fiddled with a ring on his left hand that I hadn't even noticed. "He got a promotion. We're buying a house."

Lane blew out a breath. "Good," he said, and it sounded sincere. "I'm glad for you."

"But you're right that I'm not here by chance. I have a gift for you." He smiled his friendly—*smarmy*—smile and folded his hands on the tabletop. "A research opportunity. At UGA."

Lane froze, his lips parting slightly, but no sound came out.

"Simon's promotion... he's been made dean of your old department, and they're expanding the vet program," Chad explained. "Adding more fieldwork, integrating teaching with hands-on animal care. You'd still get to teach, but you'd also have a chance to work directly with animals. Exactly what you said you wanted."

Lane's eyes flicked to me for a second, blinking rapidly. My stomach twisted.

He did that blinking thing when I offered him a second slice of cake for dessert or when he was late for work, but I started getting handsy in the shower.

It was the blink of temptation.

"You'd have access to state-of-the-art facilities," Chad went on. "More funding than you'd know what to do with. A chance to make a real impact. They're looking for someone to lead the program, and I told Simon you'd be perfect for it. You don't need to be back until this summer."

"This summer?" Lane whispered. "But..."

Kelsey returned at that moment. "Here we go! Coke for Jay. Sweet tea with lemon for Lane. And soda and lime for... the older gentleman." She set down Chad's drink, and I decided she deserved a really, really good tip.

Lane stared at the glass she'd set in front of him. "There are three lemon wedges in this," he said, surprised.

Kelsey nodded. "Annie-Ruth at the Tavern told me that's how you take your tea. Three lemons, always. Never two, never four." She giggled like she found Lane adorable... and I couldn't argue since I agreed. "Is that okay?"

"It's perfect," Lane told her with a smile. "Best thing about a small town, huh? People know you."

Kelsey nodded.

So did I.

Chad scowled.

"I'll need another minute with the menu to choose my entree," he told Kelsey curtly. Once she departed again, he turned to me. His eyes narrowed, and I knew I was not going to like whatever came next. "Jay, I want you to order whatever you want today."

I frowned. "Uh... I was planning on it. They have great rib eyes—"

"I don't want you to worry about the expense, alright? I know this place is probably a bit much for you," Chad went on pleasantly. "It's my treat."

Hand on my Coke, I froze. Had I heard him right?

The way Lane's expression had locked into a mixture of horror, anger, and misery suggested I had.

"Chad," he said, voice shaking with anger. "What the hell—?"

"Not a problem," I told Chad tightly. "I can pay my own way."

It was on the tip of my tongue to tell Chad I had more than enough money—that I could buy the dang Steak n' Bait, if such a thought ever occurred to me—but I pinched my mouth shut.

When I'd invested my last couple of thousand dollars in my friend's start-up a few years back, I'd done it because he needed the help, and I'd had it to give, not because I had any idea I'd end up wealthy. And I didn't tell folks in town that I had money, or even that I owned the Suds Barn, because I didn't want them looking at me like I ought to be one of the folks in suits at the table at the front of the restaurant—all talk, talk, talk and no action. No *fun*.

I liked cleaning cars. I liked having time to help out my friends and neighbors. I liked being Jaybird Proud.

For half a second, though, I wavered, and I wondered whether the money would make any difference to Lane. Whether it would make up for my lack of degrees and lack of refinement and lack of ambition.

Just a few hours ago, I would have sworn he wouldn't

have cared either way, but suddenly, I wasn't sure of anything...

Except that if I kept sitting here, I really was gonna pop Lane's ex-boyfriend in the mouth, and then what would happen to Lane's exciting job offer?

I was not going to ruin this for Lane.

I pushed to my feet and summoned a friendly smile. "Shoot, I just remembered I, uh... I'm not going to be able to do lunch after all."

"Oh, no." Lane stood too, eyes wide and worried. "Jay, are you—?"

"Sure. Yeah. I'm fine." I waved a hand. "Just remembered I promised I'd help... somebody with an Entwinin'... thing. I saw Chuck Gimbal out front. If I hurry, I bet I can catch a ride with him."

I gave Lane another smile, a warmer one, because none of this was his fault. None at all. He was still the handsomest, kindest man in the world. He'd told me he only wanted casual, and I hadn't entirely believed him, and that was my own doing. "I'll catch you gents later."

"I'll see you at home?" Lane asked hopefully. "Tonight?"

"Probably, yeah." I shrugged. "I live there, don't I?"

It was a funny thing how a broken heart could feel so much like a sick stomach. I took a quick detour from the lobby to the men's room, worried my breakfast was about to reappear. Fortunately, it only took a minute of me staring at my own reflection before I got my stomach back under control.

My heart was a different matter.

I didn't know if that fucker was ever gonna work properly again.

I refused to look back at the dining room as I made my

way outside. I hoped Lane was listening to Chad's business offer, if that was what he wanted. I definitely didn't want him to turn down his dream because his ex had acted like an utter asshole to his... landlord.

I wanted Lane for myself, yes. But I wanted him happy more than anything.

When I pushed open the front door of the restaurant, I grabbed my phone and texted Ava Siegel for a ride—I'd babysat for her brood on Valentine's Day, and she kept reminding me she owed me a favor as well as a Purple Heart —then found a seat on a bench behind a big Entwinin' topiary and waited for her giant minivan to appear.

This meant I had a birds'-eye view when Lane and Chad exited the restaurant.

"—an utter *jerk*, Chadwick! Honest to God. Were you this bad when we were together? Because if you were always such a genuinely awful, absolutely heartless human being and I was... was... *blind* to it, then I... I don't even know!"

Lane sounded so miserable I wanted to walk up behind him and wrap my arms around him, but I didn't think that would be helpful.

"Lane." Chad sighed. "You misinterpreted—"

"Misinterpreted *what?*" Lane demanded, sounding angrier than I'd ever heard him. "You interrupting my lunch plans? You whipping your dick out in the middle of the restaurant so you could compare it to Jay's? You insulting him because you think he doesn't make as much money as you?" His disgust was palpable. "You're insufferable, and you hurt his feelings. You owe him an apology."

Chad sighed again. "Look, I admit that I could have been nicer. But Lane, I had to be a little cruel. Think of it as an intervention."

"Oh, for fuck's sake—"

"Seriously," Chad continued. "Open your eyes and look around you, Lane. Lift your brain out of your dick and *think*. This town... this place... it's not *you*. You've got a Bachelor's in Animal Science from UT, a Master's in Veterinary Pathology from Cornell, and a Doctor of Veterinary Technology from UGA."

"I'm aware, thank you," Lane said, voice hard.

"The American Association of Veterinary Medical Colleges awarded you the Gold Standard Veterinary Excellence Award seven years ago. Two and a half years ago, you won the UGA Excellence in Veterinary Education Award. Remember the reception at the dean's house? How he said you had a bright future ahead of you?"

"I was there." Lane sounded tired now. "Of course I remember."

"And can you actually look me in the eye and tell me that man would turn down a job like the one I offered you so he could stay in some hick town and make calf's eyes at Jaybird Proud?"

I shouldn't have been listening to this conversation, and I knew it. When I was growing up, Grandma Emmaline used to tell me, "*Eavesdroppers never hear nothin' but bad news, Jaybird.*" But at that moment, a crowbar couldn't have pried me out of my hidey-hole behind the topiary.

Way deep down, beyond the pain and heartbreak, there was still a small kernel of hope inside me that Lane would pick me—and the Thicket—and tell Chad to take his stupid job and his even stupider, smarmy smile and fuck off (but politely).

I leaned forward expectantly.

I was not expecting to hear Lane's laugh ring out— hollow, yes, but still.

And I was not expecting to hear the man I loved say the words, "God. You're right. You're right, Chad. I definitely would not have."

The blood rushing in my ears meant I didn't have to hear anything else after that.

Chapter Seven

Lane

"And can you actually look me in the eye and tell me that man would turn down a job like the one I offered you so he could stay in some hick town and make calf's eyes at Jaybird Proud?" Chad demanded.

I'd gotten used to surprises since moving to Licking Thicket. No two days were ever the same here, and my life was the opposite of boring. Still, having my ex-boyfriend show up, crash my lunch date, offer me a job, and stage an intervention?

As Jay would say, "That wasn't on my bingo card."

I couldn't help but laugh, even though the situation wasn't funny.

"God. You're right. You're right, Chad. I definitely would not have," I admitted.

The Lane he'd known, the guy I'd been before moving here nine months ago, would *never*. I'd been all about having an important job title and important degrees, important connections and an important boyfriend, like being surrounded by all that importance would make *me* important too.

Fortunately, I knew better now.

I'd moved to this weird and wonderful town. I'd made friends from all walks of life. I had a career I found truly fulfilling...

And I'd met a man who showed me every day what it felt like to actually *feel* important.

I gave Chad half a second to look a little relieved and a little smug before I took a breath and continued. "But I'm not that guy anymore. Moreover, I have no interest in being that person ever again."

"Oh, Lane, come on," he sneered. "You want me to believe you've had some kind of Hallmark aha moment where you realized Lick-A-Hedge, Tennessee, is a magical place, and you suddenly have the desire to plant trees and commune with nature in the town gazebo? I know you, Lane."

I cocked my head and studied Chad. When we'd broken up over a year ago, I'd been genuinely upset. I'd believed all the bullshit he'd spouted at the end about my lack of commitment to our relationship and my emotional unavailability. I'd thought it was my fault.

Now I knew better about that too, and it was a real relief.

"Do you? What do I like on my toast?"

Chad tilted his head at me as if I was a strange creature he couldn't make out. "On your toast?"

"Yeah. You know me, you said. You just recounted every single degree I've earned and every award I've won. We were together for months. So what do I like on my toast?"

"Uh, butter?"

I thought back to the little jar of honey that was present every time Jay made me breakfast, though I'd never seen him use it himself. Chad and I had shared many breakfasts in our time together, but he'd never noticed my preferences, let alone gone to any effort on my behalf.

I grinned at him and nodded. "This explains a lot. You think you know me, Chad. But you don't. You act like you're interested in me and my future, but you're not," I said. "You wanted a partner who looked good on your arm, someone whose resume coordinated with yours. And that's okay—"

Chad's chin came up. "Excuse me? I'm a professional. An academic. It's not wrong for me to care that the man I'm with is as ambitious as I am. And I can recognize a mid-life crisis when I see one. I'm worried about you. I'm trying to be a friend to you here, Lane, despite your failures as a romantic partner—"

I shook my head. "No, you're not. You are an unfeeling, entitled elitist of the first order. You're the worst kind of snob. You're probably offering me this job because it makes you feel less guilty about how shitty you were when we broke up. You can't imagine that I'm truly happier without you. But you know what? It turns out *you* were the problem. So... thank you, Chad." I smiled. "Truly. Our breakup was the best thing you've ever done for me. Now, take me back to the clinic."

It was clear that Chad didn't know how to take my genuine gratitude, so I stopped talking and made my way to his Lexus.

The drive back to the clinic was silent and awkward. Chad made a small huff of laughter as if trying to provoke me into starting something, but I barely noticed. I truly didn't care what Chad thought of me or my choices.

Jay, on the other hand...

My stomach roiled. What the hell did Jay think now

that he'd met the unfeeling ass I'd spent a chunk of my life with? He must have lost all respect for me over the past hour, and who could blame him? Certainly not me.

I was furious with Chad for being an unfeeling, embarrassing asshole but even more furious at myself for allowing him to ruin my lunch with Jay.

I'd had a plan, damn it.

I'd told Jay *casual* after our first hookup because once I'd let down my guard and started believing all his acts of kindness were sincere, I'd been scared as fuck of just how much I liked him... and how badly I wanted him.

But from the first night, there'd been nothing truly casual about us.

The more time I spent with Jay, the more I wanted to spend. There hadn't been many nights I hadn't wanted to be with him, regardless of whether we hooked up or not.

Jay was just... *good.* And he was so much more than that. Sexy, funny, clever, energetic, empathetic, generous. Most of all, he was kind. The world needed more people like Jaybird Proud. *I* needed more of him.

And I'd set out to tell him exactly that by arranging a special meal at the Thicket's known "couples" restaurant—a lunch, since the Steak n' Bait's dinner reservations at this time of year were gobbled up months in advance—and specifically ordering their *Tot*-ally Tied Together Entwinin' Platter.

It was the kind of cheesy gesture that Thicketeers let themselves enjoy without shame, and while the old me might have scoffed, the new Lane—the one who freaking loved this town and all its sentimentality—was totally here for it.

What better way to ask Jay to make our not-casual-ness

official than by doing it in a time-honored Thicket tradition, right?

And then fucking Chad had shown up.

Chad pulled into the handicapped spot in front of the clinic door and turned toward me. "You didn't used to be this stubborn, Lane. I don't know how to make you see reason. What do you want from me?"

I laughed, though inside, I was raging. He'd shown up out of the blue without warning, acted like one of the greatest men I'd ever known was nothing but a splotch of mud on his shoe, and now he was acting like I was the unreasonable one?

I knew exactly what I wanted from him. "We're done, Chad. We're not friends, and if I didn't make this clear earlier, I already have a job I love. Please go be happy. Have a wonderful life. I truly want that for you. But don't mess with mine ever again."

I opened the car door and got out. Without a backward glance, I strode into the clinic.

My clinic.

The veterinary practice I enjoyed running with Alva, where I was proud of the work I was doing, and I was happier than I'd even realized.

When I stepped inside, Pete stopped what he was doing. "Omigosh, tell me everything. Did you really date that guy? Was that a wedding ring on his finger? Think he's in an open marriage? Think he'd be interested in a younger, slightly vertically challenged..." He frowned. "Wait, where's Jay?"

I lowered my voice and kept my eyes on Pete. "Is Chad gone?"

Pete craned his neck to see. "Yeah. He's gone."

I blew out a long breath. "Good riddance. I doubt he'll be back, but stay away from him. He's mean as fuck."

"Shit." Pete blinked. "Why'd you date him, then? Wait, don't answer that. He probably has other assets that made up for it, right?" He bounced his eyebrows. "I'll let a guy be a little mean if he's good at what he... *does*."

"He's *not* good at what he does," I said with a laugh. "He's average at what he does, and it's not worth putting up with his bullshit. He's a bunch of advanced degrees in a trench coat, pretending to be a human."

Pete nodded. "Wow."

"I'm genuinely embarrassed that I used to date him. If you'd heard the shit he said to Jay, how gross and insulting he was..." I shook my head and pressed the heels of my hands to my eyes until I saw starbursts behind my lids. "What a clusterfuck."

Pete came around the counter, locked the front door, then guided me back to the break room. "Mrs. Newman canceled. She said Sassafrass 'isn't in the mood' to be placed in her kitty carrier, which means there's nothing on the schedule for the rest of the day." He pushed me into a plastic chair and took the one beside me. "So tell me everything."

I opened my mouth to prevaricate, feeling a resurgence of the awkwardness I'd felt when I first moved here. I hadn't been used to opening up to people and trusting that they wouldn't use it against me.

But Jay had taught me differently, and I realized I was done denying my feelings for him.

Slowly, I explained the whole tale to Pete, starting with Jay's incredible acts of service, then our "casual" hookups that had quickly turned into more.

"Hunter explained the whole concept of tater-tots-as-a-symbol-of-commitment to me a few weeks ago, so I made reservations at the Steak n' Bait for me and Jay. I was going to tell him... I was going to see if..."

Pete grinned. "You were going to get him drunk on tots and ask him to go steady, weren't you?"

I closed my eyes and counted to three. "Not the phrase I was planning on using, but yes."

He nodded. "I approve. Jay's a good guy."

"The best," I said idly. "But now it's all..." I let out a breath. "Chad made me sound like an ass. He was judgmental and petty. Rude and snobbish. I can't even imagine what Jay thought. He was so offended and disgusted he wouldn't even ride back here with us."

I'd noticed on my way in that Jay's truck no longer sat in a spot way off to the side of the parking lot, where he'd parked it so as not to inconvenience anyone. That was how Jay was... unlike the jerk in the Lexus who'd pulled into a handicapped spot without a second thought.

"My plan's ruined," I whispered. "I wanted to convince Jay that... that we belonged together. Instead, that lunch showed that I'm an asshole with terrible taste in boyfriends. I wouldn't blame him if he wanted nothing more to do with me."

"Ex-boyfriends," Pete said.

I turned to look at him. "What?"

"Lane, you have terrible taste in *ex*-boyfriends," he said reasonably. "Lots of us do."

"Oh." I considered this. "But Jay was so angry and hurt. I could tell, even though he tried not to make a scene. And he probably blames me—he *should*—because it was my fault Chad was even here—"

Pete raised a hand and cut me off. "Do you think Jay is stupid?"

Riled as I was from the disastrous lunch, I didn't stop to consider what Pete was really asking. I immediately bristled from head to toe and stood up so fast the legs of the chair *screeched* against the linoleum floor.

"Are you serious right now, Pete Winchell? Jaybird Proud is maybe the smartest person I've ever met! If you think for one second that's not true just because he doesn't have a bunch of fucking diplomas on his wall, then you'd better think again. Jay is talented. He can fix nearly everything. And he knows people. He *cares*. He's openhearted, and open-minded, and generous, and..."

I trailed off when I saw Pete's grin.

"Uh-huh. I know how smart he is, which is how I know he's not going to blame you for Chad. And... frankly, I think you're the one who's a little dense when it comes to Jay. He knows you're a good guy," Pete said kindly. "He likes you. Like, *a lot*. No landlord brings their tenant a snack every single day, Lane. Not even in the Thicket. Not even if that landlord is Jaybird Proud. I'd bet money he feels the same way you do. You just need to talk to him."

I flopped back in the chair, completely out of sorts. I couldn't stop thinking of Jay's face when he'd gotten up from the table at the restaurant—the tightness of his mouth and the bleakness in his eyes. The idea of Jay being hurt, of me causing that hurt, made me want to vomit. "He was upset, Pete. I've never seen him bolt out of a place that fast before. I should have never invited Chad to lunch."

Pete shrugged. "You'll explain and apologize. So what if you're not perfect? Jay's pretty down-to-earth. He wouldn't go for someone who wanted to be perfect all the time."

Pete's words made something click in my brain. I thought about my time with Chad. Our glossy, picture-perfect life in Athens. From the outside, it had seemed enviable, but inside, it had been stifling.

I'd been running on fumes, chasing a vision of success—a level of perfection—that was as hollow as Chad's compliments.

"I don't want a perfect life," I murmured, processing this new realization. "Perfection's not attainable or sustainable."

"Nope. Not any fun either," Pete agreed. "Jaybird Proud, though. He's tons of fun."

I inhaled deeply, remembering the time back in March when the weather was still a bit chilly but with the first hint of spring in the air. Jay had decided to host a "Firepit Feast" in the backyard, complete with a bonfire, homemade chili... and outdoor charades.

"BYOB," he'd told the guests. "Bring your own blankets."

When it was Quinn Champion's turn to play, the man had taken one look at the selection on his piece of paper, shrugged, and immediately started running around the yard while flapping his hands, ducking his head, and jumping over furniture.

"You're a... a chicken," Diesel Partridge had guessed. "Throwing a tantrum because the Wi-Fi in the Poultry Palace went out."

"You're... Beyoncé's least-coordinated backup dancer?" Brooks Johnson had offered.

"You're... little Beau Siegel after gorging himself on leftover Halloween candy," Brooks's husband, Mal, had thrown in, laughing when Ava Siegel—Beau's mom—slapped his leg.

"You're... *you*, the morning you managed to buy Taylor Swift tickets," Quinn's husband, Champ, had said blandly.

Quinn had stopped flapping and given his husband a raised-eyebrow glare that suggested Champ would be paying for that tease later... though Champ's answering smirk had said he wouldn't mind one bit.

"Nah. You're Indiana Jones when he's escaping from the Temple of Doom," Jay had said with utter confidence. "Easy peasy."

Quinn had thrown up his hands. "*Thank* you, Jay," he'd said, breathless from exertion. "Finally. At least *someone* around here understands me."

"Jay *is* fun," I told Pete, unable to keep a smile off my face. "He's fun, and he's *kind*. And I love him for it."

"Love?" Pete said, grinning and bouncing his eyebrows again. "You gonna make him a wreath, Doc Lane? Wrap your vines of love all around him?"

My stomach twisted even as I waved a hand. "I'm gonna try. I made him a wreath a while ago. It's terrible, but it's done. I mean. Kind of. Overdone, maybe. I tried fixing it a few times, and it didn't get any better." I scraped my upper lip with my teeth. "It's a lot of pressure, making a wreath for the Thicket's Entwinin' expert."

Pete *tsk*'d. "It's the gesture, Lane. Not the craftsmanship. And you're not about perfection anymore."

I remembered Jay the night he'd introduced me to Disco Dave, telling me that nobody expected perfection in an Entwinin' wreath because "the real perfection is the love the maker has for their Entwined."

Loving Jaybird Proud was the only kind of perfection I was interested in anymore.

I nodded. "Thanks, Pete. That helps."

"Talk to him, Doc. And get on out of here. If anyone shows up needing their anal glands expressed, I'm your man."

I let out a laugh and headed home as quickly as possible.

I was surprised to find that most of the afternoon had passed while I'd been talking with Pete. When I got back to Jay's house, the lights in his garage workshop were on, casting a warm glow into the dusky yard.

I knocked on the open garage door, stepping inside when he didn't respond. Jay was hunched over his workbench on a stool, his hands busy weaving wisteria vines into a wreath. He didn't greet me with his usual "Howdy, neighbor." He didn't even look up.

"Hey," I called, suddenly hesitant.

"Hey. Thought you'd be a while," he said without turning around. "Catching up with Chad and all that. Getting the scoop on your new job. You looked real excited."

I blinked. *Had* I? Maybe, for half a second. The research position was the sort of thing that would have excited me... before I'd figured out what, and who, I really wanted.

I stepped closer. "Do *you* think I should take it?"

His shoulders lifted and lowered, the faded denim of his shirt covered in bits and pieces of dried vine. "Why wouldn't you? Sounds like a good opportunity. You'll get to spend time with the kind of folks you like to spend time with. Folks who are smart, like you. You deserve it. H-happy for you."

Jay didn't sound happy in the slightest, and that knowledge gave me courage.

I stepped closer again, wanting nothing more than to lean my face into his neck and inhale deeply, apologize, and beg for forgiveness.

"Too bad I turned it down, then, huh?"

He pivoted on the stool until he faced me, his expression uncharacteristically shuttered. My chest ached with the knowledge I was partially responsible for it.

"You...? But I thought... Chad said that job was exactly what you wanted."

"It might have been, once. But..." I pressed my lips together for a moment as if in thought. "I love my job here. I love house calls to Dunn's farm just to find out Bernadette the pig is unhappy with her new nail polish color. I love watching kids like Jolly Parsons bring in the new puppy she earned with her hard work walking other dogs in the neighborhood. And I love standing in line at Henson's Grocery, overhearing that you donated a brand-new parka to the old coat drive and knowing it's because you still can't bring yourself to get rid of a coat I wore one time, months ago."

Jay's eyes widened. "You heard about that?"

I stepped closer and used my thumb to gently brush a piece of dirt off his cheek. "I did. And I thought, 'Now, *that* is a guy I want to spend time with. That is a guy who's *smart* 'cause he knows what's really important.'"

He blinked, and I almost laughed.

"You make me feel so cared for, Jay. So understood. So *liked*. And I set up a whole lunch at the Steak n' Bait so I could tell you how much it means to me..." I grimaced. "But then I had to go and ruin it with an accidental assholering."

The edges of Jay's lips quirked up. "You're the one with the big vocabulary, but I don't think that's a word, fancy pants."

That tiny glimmer of a smile did things to my insides. "I am so sorry about today. The things Chad said... the way he treated you... It was disgusting, and I told him so. I'm ashamed I ever dated him and even more ashamed to think I might have once acted like that—"

"Hey, now." Jay's smile disappeared, and he clapped a

hand over my mouth. "Stop talkin' silly talk. You could never, Lane Desmond. Not possible." He shook his head angrily. "I used to wonder what kind of fool your ex must've been to give you up... Now I'm just sorry you wasted a second of your time with him."

If Jay wouldn't listen to my words, maybe I could tell him how I felt with my actions.

I removed his hand from my mouth, then leaned down and pressed my lips to his.

He made a muffled sound of surprise and appreciation that quickly turned into a low groan as he deepened the kiss. Jay's hands moved to my hips, pulling me down until I was straddled over his legs on the metal stool. I arched into him, pressing my thickening cock against the bulge in his pants.

"Come upstairs with me," I murmured against his mouth. "I want you more than you could ever know."

Jay pulled back and studied me. "You sure about this?"

I cupped his face and met his eyes. "As sure as you are that Partridge Pit's barbecue is better than Susie Dupree's."

He frowned again. "Well, but... that's just a *fact*, Lane."

I nodded. Jay had once talked for twenty minutes straight about the Pit's secret-recipe sauce. "I know."

"And their commitment to offering vegan options—"

"I know, baby."

"And they make their own pickles, which—"

I kissed him again because I couldn't help it.

"Jaybird," I said, laughing. "Do you want to stand here talking about barbecue all night, or do you want to go upstairs and... rattle your train for me?"

Jay didn't hesitate. He jumped up, turned off the lights, and shut the garage door behind us.

After leading him up to my place, I took my time

undressing him, dropping open-mouthed kisses on every newly exposed inch of him as I went. By the time I had Jay naked on my bed, I was short of breath from wanting him.

"You're so fucking beautiful," I said, eating him up with my eyes.

Jay's body was lean but strong, thanks to a lifetime of physical jobs. I was obsessed with those arms he displayed on a daily basis, with his broad shoulders and his taut stomach. I wanted to lick every inch of him, connect the dots across his freckled chest with my tongue and turn them into pictures, to kiss him until he couldn't see straight.

But more than any of that, I wanted to make Jaybird feel as seen and as loved as he made me feel every day. "What would make you feel good tonight?"

He huffed out a laugh. "This. All of this. What you're already doing."

I pressed a kiss to his shoulder. "What else?"

His eyes darkened. "I want to fuck you, Lane."

My stomach tightened with need and desire. We'd talked about it before, but for the past few months, we'd been too eager to get off with quick handjobs and blowjobs to need anything more.

"Yes," I breathed.

Jay shifted us quickly until I was flat on my back and all of those muscles were pinning me down. My heart rate picked up as I imagined him thrusting inside me. Fuck, I wanted that.

"You going to relax?" he asked with a teasing glint in his eyes. "You're practically vibrating." He moved his hand down to run a finger over my hole.

I groaned.

The room was warm, the soft glow of the bedside lamp casting Jay's shoulders in golden light as he leaned over me.

His weight pressed against me, grounding me, and I couldn't look away from the way he was watching me—like I was the only thing that mattered in the world.

"Lane," he murmured, his voice rough, reverent. He brushed his thumb across my cheek, his other hand settling on my hip. "Are you sure?"

I nodded, my throat tight. I tried to cut the tension with a joke. "Sure I want you at least half as much as Disco Dave did when he first arrived."

Jay's gaze softened, and he kissed me again, slow and deliberate. His lips were warm, his beard rough against my skin as he trailed kisses down my neck, over my collarbone, and lower still. Each touch left a trail of heat in its wake, every flick of his tongue pulling quiet gasps from my lips.

His hands were everywhere—firm and steady as he guided me into place, my body open beneath him. I shivered as his fingers trailed down my stomach, skimming over sensitive skin before settling between my legs.

"You're perfect," he murmured, almost to himself. Then he glanced at me with flushed cheeks. "Prettier than a peacock."

I huffed out a laugh, my head falling back against the pillow. "Pretty sure that's going on the list for cheesiest line anyone's ever used during sex."

Jay shook his head, grinning. "Give it time. I can get cheesier."

I wanted to give it time. I wanted to have all the time in the world with him.

His fingers slipped lower, circling me in a way that made my breath hitch. He took his time, his movements coaxing me open until I was panting, my hips lifting into his touch.

"Jay," I breathed, gripping his arms. "Please."

He leaned down, brushing his lips against my ear. "I don't want to hurt you," he said, his voice barely above a deep whisper. "Tell me if I do."

"You won't," I promised, my voice shaking. "I trust you."

He kissed me again, slower this time, his lips lingering on mine as he reached for the bottle of lube from the night-stand drawer. I heard the faint click of the cap, the cool sensation of the gel slicking his fingers before he pressed them against me.

I gasped at the first touch, my body tensing instinctively before I forced myself to relax. Jay's hand was steady, his voice low and soothing as he murmured soft reassurances against my temple.

"That's it," he said, breath warm against my skin. "Relax, sweetheart."

When he finally slid inside me, the stretch was intense, a mix of discomfort and pleasure that left me breathless. Jay stilled, his body trembling with restraint as he gave me time to adjust, his hands gripping my hips like they were the only thing tethering him to the moment.

"Lane," he said again, his voice breaking. "You feel so... God, you feel amazing."

My fingers tightened in the sheets, my body arching into his. "Yes, fuck," I managed, my voice a little desperate. "Jay."

He moved, his hips rolling forward in a rhythm that sent sparks of pleasure racing up my spine. The discomfort faded quickly, replaced by a growing heat that built with every thrust, every brush of his skin against mine.

"Is this okay?" he asked, his voice strained. "Am I—"

"Don't you dare stop," I gasped, cutting him off.

Jay's movements grew faster, more urgent, but he never lost the tenderness in his touch. His lips found mine again, swallowing my gasps and moans as he pushed me closer to the edge. Every thrust hit a spot deep inside me that made my vision blur, my body trembling as the pressure built to an unbearable peak.

I thought about how affectionate he was with me, how protective. How much he always put my pleasure above his own. How much I trusted him. Emotion overwhelmed me. I wanted to say something to tell him what I was feeling, but I was still scared my confession would somehow screw things up.

"Jay, I—" I started, but the words were swallowed by a cry as I came undone beneath him, the pleasure ripping through me like a wave. My hands gripped his back, nails digging into his skin as I shattered in his arms.

Jay wasn't far behind, his rhythm faltering as he groaned my name, his head dropping to my shoulder as he followed me over the edge.

We stayed like that for a long moment, our bodies tangled, our breaths mingling in the quiet. Jay pressed a soft kiss to my shoulder before rolling to the side, pulling me with him.

"You good?" he asked, his voice low and rough.

I nodded, curling into his chest. "That display more than lived up to the train rattling."

He chuckled softly, his hand trailing up and down my back. "Good. Because I don't think I can move for a while."

I smiled, letting myself relax against him. In his arms, I felt whole, complete, like every jagged piece of me had finally found its place.

I'd been patient, just like Disco Dave had learned to be... and now, finally, I'd found my mate.

And for the first time in a long time, I wasn't afraid of what came next.

Chapter Eight

Jay

A few hours after Lane fell asleep, I had to admit defeat. Sleep wasn't coming for me. I had too much on my mind.

As much as I'd enjoyed every minute of my evening with Lane, and as relieved as I was to hear he wasn't taking Chad's job offer and moving away, I had to remind myself there hadn't been any kind of declaration in his words or actions.

Lane had said he was happy in the Thicket, that he felt good and cared for when he was with me, and that he appreciated it so much he'd gone to the trouble of setting us up a nice lunch.

All that was great.

Really, genuinely great.

Not only did it make my chest squeeze that he'd gone to the trouble of showing me his appreciation—though Lane was always thoughtful that way—his decision to turn down the Georgia job meant we could keep doing what we'd been doing for the past couple of months: spending time together, casual and easy, for as long as he stayed in town.

That should have been enough, I knew. For a small-town guy like me, keeping someone who shined as bright as Lane Desmond in my life in *any* capacity should have been enough. It'd be greedy to ask for more. But *damn*, when I was holding Lane in my arms and watching him sleep, fresh from feeling him come undone on my cock, I felt all kinds of greedy.

I wanted more with Lane.

If I was being really honest, I wanted... everything.

I wanted commitment and love and Entwinin'.

I wanted a wedding at the town event barn and for us to raise the next generation of Licking Thicket Bovine wide receivers (or cute little mathletes, or animal lovers, or artists, I didn't care) together.

I wanted us to watch Disco Dave's great-grandfowl strutting around our yard.

I wanted forever.

But it wasn't up to me.

I carefully disentangled myself from Lane's bed and stood, watching with a grin as he rolled into my warm spot—as per usual—and burrowed under his blankets.

Tomorrow was the Entwinin', and I had a metric shit-ton of stuff still to do, so I snuck out quietly and made my way down to my workshop. There were a few things I wanted to add to the wreath I'd made Lane, and I needed to get it done before finishing up the other projects on my workbench.

The encounter with Chad and then my conversation with Lane afterward rolled through my head as I took a seat on my stool. Now that my anger and hurt feelings were mostly soothed—and, okay, now that I'd come my brains out and held Lane tight for a while—I could finally think clearly.

The wisteria vines bit into my palms as I twisted them tighter, forming new additions to Lane's wreath.

Lane had said he was happy here, and if he'd said it, he meant it. The man I loved was no liar. I knew he enjoyed working with Alva and Pete, he enjoyed getting to work with animals rather than just teaching about them, and he enjoyed getting to know his "patients" and their owners. After last night, I knew he had feelings for me. I knew he cared about me.

But that wasn't the same as wanting to be together for the long haul. And from all the reminiscing Chad had done, it was clear Lane had been happy in his last life too... until he hadn't.

If there was one thing Chad's visit had made me realize on a gut-deep level, it was that Lane's world was much bigger than mine. Now that I knew what kind of situation he'd given up to move here, I couldn't help wondering how likely it was that someone as smart and talented as Lane would stay in Tennessee permanently, giving Mrs. Moore's Persian cat yet another claw trim ("because Doc Lane has a real talent for soothing my Susannah's delicate feline nerves") and spending time with a man who genuinely enjoyed working at a car wash, when he could find himself a high-paying job in a bigger town and a man he'd be proud to have on his arm.

I truly didn't know.

I wasn't without hope—there were plenty of couples in Licking Thicket, including Dunn and Tucker, and my own cousin Charlie and his Hunter, where someone had moved in from a big city and decided to stick around—but the odds seemed low. I was a lucky man, but I didn't know if a person could get quite that lucky.

And that was... well, I couldn't make myself say it was okay, even in my own mind, because it wasn't.

Losing Lane would hurt worse than when I'd been team captain and the Bovines had lost the football championship in double overtime during the last game of my senior year. Worse than the time I'd managed to have the stomach flu and the regular flu and a sprained rib, all at once. Worse than anything I'd ever felt.

But that didn't mean I wouldn't love him while I had him. I'd never understood the sense of cutting yourself off from caring about other people just because they might eventually leave—that would be like never eating ice cream because you might someday be lactose intolerant or never learning to walk because you might end up with gout like old Herman Wanamaker.

In fact, the opposite was true. I wanted to love Lane as hard as I could for as long as I could. I wanted to love him like it was my full-time job. I wanted that man to be so loved up his whole body glowed like a neon sign. I wanted to hold up a mirror and show Lane his own worth until joy burst out of his stomach like that creature in the *Alien* movies and—

Shit.

I blinked down at the wreath in my hand, finding I'd managed to twist a vine into a tiny feral alien just waiting for Sigourney Weaver to come along.

I sighed. Hopefully, Lane wouldn't notice since there were plenty of other things for him to see on the wreath.

I wiped a hand across my brow, smearing dirt over my skin, and got back to work. This wreath needed to be perfect. For Lane. For the man who deserved everything.

The smell of fresh blooms filled the air, mingling with

the scent of sawdust and the faint tang of Georgia clay I'd used to create the base for my Georgia Bulldog wreath. He'd been a professor at UGA and had spent a number of years on campus and in the community. It was silly, probably, but I wanted him to have pieces of where he came from and to show him just how well it coordinated with the place he'd ended up.

I'd also worked some tiny wooden carvings of animals into the vines—his patients, the ones I'd seen him care for with that steady, quiet determination. I'd shaped a small peacock feather out of wire and tucked it near the top, a nod to Disco Dave and the day Lane had looked at me like I was more than just his landlord. I'd crafted a honey jar and added that, too, as a symbol of how much I loved our mornings together.

My hands moved on autopilot, but my thoughts ran wild, picking apart every stupid dream I'd let myself have over the past six months. Lane smiling at me over breakfast. Lane's hand brushing mine as we wrangled Disco Dave and his crew. Lane kissing me like I mattered.

I smiled to myself. As much as I gave Lane, he gave me back a hundredfold in the simple pleasure of his company, the warmth of his presence, his daily kindnesses, and the way he let me care for him, not because he necessarily needed it but because he understood *I* did.

The two of us could sustain each other for a lifetime, if he'd let us, and I wanted the wreath to show that too. I wanted him to see the hope and possibility of a life with me. I wanted him to see that my heart was his with no strings attached—no contracts and no down payment required.

This wreath was a story. His story. Our story. And if Lane did decide to leave someday, I wanted him to have this wreath to take with him so he'd remember that somebody in the world saw him, understood him, appreciated him... and loved him.

I stepped back, wiping my hands on my jeans as I stared at my creation. It wasn't just the best Entwinin' wreath I'd ever made; it was the best thing I'd ever made, period, and I was pretty damn proud of it.

But it occurred to me that I didn't quite know how to give it to him.

Some folks liked to make a big production of giving their wreaths right in the middle of town at the Entwinin' festival, and I understood that. Part of the fun was being able to show the world how much love and pride you had for your Entwined. All the displays of affection, all the positivity and joy from seeing other people happy... it was energizing and uplifting.

On the other hand, plenty of folks preferred to give their wreaths privately—an opportunity for a sweet and special moment between sweethearts or friends—and I understood that too.

But what did you do when your Entwined had said he wanted *casual* and your wreath practically shouted *I'm in love with you*? What did you do when you wanted your Entwined to know how very special he was, but you didn't want him to feel awkward that he didn't have a wreath for you or pressured to love you back?

I turned off the lights and locked the workshop behind me. I climbed the stairs to Lane's apartment and laid his wreath on the Welcome Mat, propped against the door where he'd find it in the morning. That way, the wreath didn't have to mean anything more than Lane wanted it to, and he didn't have to worry about responding in any kind of way in front of me.

But when I went home and climbed into my bed to snag

a few hours of sleep, the night felt heavier than usual, like the weight of all the things I wasn't telling Lane was pressing down on my chest.

Eventually—soon, maybe even tomorrow after the festival—I needed to tell him how I felt.

I needed to ask him if there was any possibility the novelty of living in the Thicket would wear off one day... and, if not, would he want to make a go of it with a simple country boy like me?

———

I woke up only two hours later and packed up my truck with the wreaths I'd made, hoping the noise from the engine wouldn't wake Lane too early.

The first several deliveries went by quickly. After seeing several sleepy faces light up with excitement when I showed them their custom wreaths, my mood had improved. As the morning wore on and my truck got emptier with each visit, I felt myself relaxing. This was my town, these were my people, and their optimism was contagious.

I loved the Entwinin'. It was like Valentine's Day but with a ton more authenticity and the social acceptance of expressing love and affection for friends and neighbors the same way we did for our romantic loves.

It was a holiday of celebrating others, celebrating community, celebrating togetherness.

When I finally finished my deliveries and made it into town, the sun had burned off the morning chill, and it had turned into a gorgeous spring day. The square was alive with music and laughter, wreaths strung from every post and hanging from shop doors. Kids ran by with sticky fingers and wide grins while couples walked hand in hand, sharing soft smiles and whispered promises.

I walked toward the center of the action, enjoying the people I'd known my whole life celebrating love in all its forms like it was the most natural thing in the world.

Because it was.

Maybe my midnight crisis had been my insecurity talking. Maybe I wasn't giving Lane enough credit to know what he wanted. He'd told me he was happy in the Thicket. Now, in the light of day and around all of the best of what made my town the most special place on Earth, I could see it. Why *wouldn't* he love it here? I sure did.

"Jaybird, sweetheart!" My grandma Emmaline walked hand-in-hand with Amos Nutter, the man she still called her *beau*, though they'd been Proud-Nutters since their marriage a couple of years back. "Happy Entwinin' to you!"

I grinned back at her before dodging a few racing kids to peck her on the cheek. "And to you. How'd you like your miniature Bovine wreath, Amos?" I asked.

Grandma's hands were too knotted up with arthritis to be able to make her own wreaths anymore, but I was more than happy to create anything she wanted to her very specific, detailed instructions.

Amos pulled his khaki jacket open to display the eight-inch wreath strung from a rope around his neck like a pendant and nestled against his heart. "Best damned cow I ever saw," he said, reaching for my hand. "And considering I once showed Rocket Ranger Rosita at the state championships, that's saying quite a bit. You do good vine, son."

I shook his hand, feeling strangely proud. "Glad to hear it."

"And did you see my special message for your grandmother this morning?"

I nodded. "Sure did, Amos. Couldn't miss it."

Amos's thin chest puffed up. "Took me forever to get those cows lined up to spell out 'ENTWINE ME, EMMALINE PROUD NUTTER.'"

The messages Amos painted on his herd had become so legendary in the Thicket folks came from surrounding towns on festival days just to see them.

But somehow, Amos never seemed to realize that his cows didn't stay where he put them.

This morning, when I'd passed his grazing field out by the highway, half a dozen cars had been pulled over so people could take cow selfies... and most of the herd had been spelling out PUT TWIN MEN IN ME EMALINE, while the others had their asses turned toward the road.

Still, it was the thought that counted, right?

"It was a... a beautiful tribute to your love," I told Amos solemnly.

Several other people approached me to thank me for my work on their wreaths and for the Entwinin' archway I'd created for the grandstand podium. "The kids are almost finished adding the wildflowers to it, and then the mayor will get the dancing started," I heard Lurleen Jackson telling Latonya Henson. I glanced over to see the archway overflowing with clumps of fresh spring flowers. Seeing it in a riot of colors made my heart swell.

If only Lane was there, I could point it out to him. But I hadn't seen him yet, which meant he'd probably gotten caught up at work with an emergency. He knew what a big deal the Entwinin' was in theory, but I couldn't wait to see him experience the real thing for himself.

The guys from Champion Security stood off to one side,

talking and joking around while enjoying Quinn Champion's spiked Love Punch. I wandered over to say hello to Kandi Nutter, who was hanging on to their every word.

"You'll never believe the wreath Hux made Kev. It's non-binary... which is weird because I thought *Jordan* was non-binary," she said in a stage whisper.

Jordan huffed out a laugh. "It's binary *code*, Kandi. You know, the language computers use? Kev's a computer geek, so he's all up in his feels about it. It's how you say I love you in computer speak."

Kev shot moony eyes at Hux. "It's naughtier than I love you. He spelled out something incredibly... um... inappropriate. And Huxley is going to get very, very lucky later because of it."

Hux wrapped a proprietary arm around Kev's waist. "As lucky as *you* got when you showed me your Horn this morning?" Seeing my startled look, he explained, "Kev managed to twine a wreath in our video game, using wisteria from our own homestead. I literally didn't know you could do that."

Kev blushed. "You can if you're friends with the programmers at *Horn of Glory* and get them to create a limited-time Jasper Huxley Entwinin' expansion pack." He shrugged. "I just wanted you to know how special you are to me."

Christ, I hoped Lane looked half as pleased when he saw my wreath. Made me kind of wish I'd been there to see his face.

I turned to ask Quinn what kind of wreath Champ made for him when I heard a shout.

"Jaybird Proud! I cannot believe you."

I froze. Lane's voice cut through the crowd like a spotlight, and he didn't sound pleased.

Suddenly, it seemed every eye in the Thicket was on me. I turned, and there he was, standing in the middle of the square, holding my wreath in his hands.

"I've been looking for you everywhere," he said loud enough for everyone to hear. His chest heaved as if he was out of breath, and his hair stuck out wildly.

I'd never seen him like this before, not Lane the polished professional or Lane the quiet guy who watched me from across the table like he was trying to figure me out. This Lane looked... riled up. And determined.

Shit. Had he felt the super un-casual wreath was a breach of our agreement? Had he felt pressured despite my best efforts? Did he really want to do this in public?

I took a step back, but he kept coming closer, the crowd parting around him like they knew something big was about to happen.

"How could you leave this on my doorstep?" he demanded, holding out the wreath I'd made him. "What in the world were you thinking?"

My mouth went dry, and my face heated to a million degrees. I'd worried about him taking it wrong, but I hadn't imagined he'd be quite this angry about it.

"I... I..." I swallowed hard. Even angry, the man was the most gorgeous thing I'd ever seen... and since I'd spent my whole life experiencing the wonders of the Thicket, that was saying something. The way I felt for him was beautiful too, even if he didn't feel the same. "I was thinking I wanted you to know how much I care about you, Lane Desmond. But it's okay if you don't feel the same," I hurried to add. "I swear. I don't expect anything—"

"Well, maybe you *should*."

Lane pulled another wreath out from his back pocket and held it up. The thing was crooked and messy as hell, not like it had been thrown together haphazardly, but more like it had been overworked and re-twined by clumsy fingers until it was mangled.

He thrust it toward me, and my heart stopped. "I made you this," he said. "It's not as beautiful as yours, but it's the best I could do. The very best, because you deserve my very best, Jay, and I want to give it to you. Even if you *did* leave a wreath on my doorstep instead of giving it to me in person."

"Lane," I breathed. I stepped toward him to take the wreath from his hand. It was made with the thin, whippy vines, the ones you had to source weeks before the Entwinin' before they were all gone.

And it was in the shape of a piece of bow tie pasta.

"This is the most perfect thing I ever saw," I said, meaning every word.

"Good. Because..." Lane cast a quick glance around, aware of everyone's eyes on him. He cleared his throat and stood up straighter. "Because I love you, Jaybird Proud, and this Entwinin' wreath represents what I love about you most: your generous spirit and the way you care for others. You are the epitome of love, Jay. You might not say it, but you *show* it. You display your love like peacock feathers. You live the spirit of the Entwinin' every day of your life."

There was a mix of gasps and *awws* from the people around us.

Lane blushed harder. "I love how much you love working at the Suds Barn. I love that you give yourself wholeheartedly to everything you do. And I love the way you take care of people. Whether it's taking extra care with Penelope Jackson's wheelchair ramp at the car wash, checking on Skeets Miller's moody furnace, leaving Italian Gentleman on my doorstep after I've had a long day, or letting a bunch of peacocks take over your yard, you are always looking out for others. You are everything good in the world, and you deserve to have someone looking out for you too. I *want* you to expect things from me. I want you to Entwine me. I want you to..." His face was red all the way to the tips of his ears. "Go steady with me, Jaybird."

I stared at him. He'd said a lot of words, and I hoped I'd remember them all, but to be honest, my mind had short-circuited after the first and most important bit. "You... love me?"

Someone in the crowd muttered, "I didn't know you could leave someone gentlemen from any country on their doorstep. Is that Instacart or Uber Eats?"

Lane shot me a grin that said he'd heard the comment and wanted to share his amusement with me. Like he enjoyed this town and its wacky residents as much as I did. "I do, Jay. So much."

I turned the wreath over, studying the intricate knots. Suddenly, the little nicks and cuts on Lane's hands these past few weeks made sense. I couldn't believe he'd been working on this, for *me*, for so long.

The wreath swam in front of my eyes a little bit, and my cheeks felt damp. "I can't... I've never... Are you sure?"

Lane seemed to understand what I was asking. He stepped closer and lowered his voice so only I could hear. "Baby, I'm positive." He lifted his hands to my face, and his thumbs brushed away my tears. "You're enough, Jay. You always were, and you always will be. I'm the one who's worried that I'm not enough for you."

"What?" My eyes snapped to his, my tears forgotten. "How could you worry about that?"

"Uh, because you haven't told me you love me yet?"

"Oh!" God, I couldn't believe I hadn't said the words out loud, despite how hard I'd been thinking them for months. "I love you! I love you so much. Of course I do." My cheeks ached from the size of my grin. I didn't think. I didn't stop to worry or doubt or second-guess. I just moved. My hands were on him, pulling him closer, and then I kissed him—hard and desperate, like I needed him to feel everything I'd just confessed.

The crowd erupted in cheers and applause, but all I could hear was the sound of Lane's breath mixing with mine. It was the kind of kiss we'd remember years from now when we thought back to the Entwinin' declaration we'd made.

When we finally broke apart, Lane was smiling at me like I was the only thing in the world he wanted. Like I was the prettiest peacock in the flock. Like I was the one he'd chosen.

People surged around us. Their comments ranged from speculation that we'd simply been overcome by the spirit of the season to comments like Pete's "It's about damned time." I didn't have much care about any of that since I was too busy soaking in the commitment Lane had made by ensuring his declaration was so public, so permanent that I'd truly believe it.

"I have a confession," I whispered. "I, uh... I don't just work at the Suds Barn. I... I kinda own the place?"

Lane's eyes widened. "Really?"

"Yeah. Long story, and I promise I'll tell you all of it, but—"

"Oh, who cares about that?" Ava Siegel said, waving a hand in the air while holding a baby on her hip with the other. "We're so happy you two found each other!"

Amos tilted his chin down. "While I can think of a better way of declaring your love in this town, I have to say I'm happy to have a vet in the family, yes I am. Old

Clarabelle isn't carrying her letter boards the way she used—"

"Oh, hush," Grandma said, grinning at us as she tucked her hand into Amos's elbow. "We're pleased as punch to have you in the family, Lane, because you're *you*. And Jaybird deserves someone who recognizes how special he is. Even if you don't know how to twine a wreath worth a dang. Is that a butterfly? Because it's missing antennae."

His eyes never moving from my face, Lane pressed his lips together like he was trying not to laugh.

Ava stepped closer and looked at the mangled bow tie wreath.

I blinked. Now that she mentioned it... it did kind of look like a butterfly without antennae. "Huh," I said, turning it around. "It's multifaceted."

Amos *tsk*'d. "It's a right mess is what it is. You need to give that boy some lessons in twinin' a vine, Jaybird. He needs some help."

In the circle of my arms, Lane's shoulders shook like he was about to erupt with laughter.

"I like him just the way he is," I assured him.

Amos shrugged. "Eh, suit yourself," he said before wandering off, asking Grandma what kind of discount he should expect on the friends and family plan at the clinic and whether or not his "new grandson" Doc Lane would do a bulk deal on bovine house calls.

Lane lost the battle he'd been waging and laughed out loud. The pure joy of the sound made me feel even giddier than I already was.

Still, I couldn't help asking, "You sure you're ready for this, Lane?"

As the noise of the festival wrapped around us again, Lane leaned in, his forehead resting against mine. "You're stuck with me now," he whispered, wrapping his arms around my neck.

And despite growing up in Licking Thicket, despite loving every single thing about the place and never doubting for an instant that this was where I belonged... with Lane's arms around me, for the first time, I truly felt like I'd found my home.

Epilogue

Jay

I PUT the finishing touches on the mural and stood back to admire the finished product. Bright, jewel-toned colors spread out in a fan across the far wall of the nursery. Lane was going to lose his mind when I finally revealed it to him.

Even though we'd only been married for eight months, we'd been together for two and a half years. It felt like longer in some ways, and in others, it felt like we'd only just met.

The way my stomach still clenched when he walked in a room, the look in his eyes when he noticed me staring at him in the morning—because watching the man sleep never got old—and the fact I still learned something new about him every day made it feel like we were still new together. But then there was the deep, long-term knowing that sometimes made me wonder if we'd been together so long it had spanned multiple lifetimes.

"You ever coming out?" Lane called through the closed door. "Because I just got a mysterious text from SaraCate."

I quickly wrapped my wet paintbrush in plastic wrap

and silently promised it I'd be back to properly clean it later. "Coming! Get away from the door, and no peeking!"

His muttered grumbles faded as he walked away. I took one last look at the giant pair of peacocks standing protectively over their tiny peahen before turning out the light and sneaking out of the room. All I had left was to put the furniture in place and accessorize before I could show Lane what I'd been working on.

"What'd she say?" I asked as I walked into our bedroom, yanking off my painting shirt. "She need a foot rub? Takeout?" I hesitated. "More pork rinds? Because if that's the case, we're going to have to say something. All that salt and fat cannot be good for—"

I looked up and noticed my husband staring at his phone. He'd gone deathly pale. "She's... she's at the hospital."

"Fuck, what happened? Is she hurt? Was she in an accident?"

Lane glanced up at me. "Babe. She's having the baby! Our baby! She's at the hospital *having our baby*."

I stared at him. "But... it's not time! We're not due for two more weeks."

He huffed out a laugh and started moving. "If there's one thing I've learned since moving to the Thicket, it's that things happen in their *own* time, whether it's peacocks mating, or us falling in love, or Memsy Blake finally taking down her holiday lights in July. It's not SaraCate's first kid. Maybe her body decided it was done, and it's evicting our daughter. Maybe it's a full moon. Who knows? But..." He spun toward me, eyes wide. "Jay, it's happening. We're having a baby!"

Poor Lane had been squawking and flapping his arms, running around in a circle between the dresser, the closet, and the nightstand but not actually packing anything. He reminded me of Disco Dave when we threw a handful of blueberries in his habitat.

"We already have a bag packed," I reminded him, pointing to the backpack in the corner. "Grab that while I put on clean clothes."

"How are you so calm? You've been panicking this entire time, and now that I finally need you to panic with me, you're... chill? Babe, what the fuck?"

I wasn't chill. Not one bit. Inside, I was worse than Disco Dave. I was a collection of drunken kittens, stumbling around but still happy as shit. But if my steady husband was panicking, the world didn't have room for anyone else to panic too.

After yanking a clean shirt on and stepping into my running shoes, I pulled out my phone and texted SaraCate back on the group chat.

Me: *On our way. What do you need?*

I shoved the phone back in my pocket and reached for Lane's hand. "C'mon. We gotta go."

His hand was clammy with nerves. "We should have never done this," he said breathily. "We... we're not ready. We... we don't know what we're doing. They're never going to let us take her home. We don't qualify."

I tried not to laugh. "Nobody qualifies, honey. And now might be a good time to remind you that you actually have a medical degree, which puts you a fair way ahead of the rest of us."

"I know how to castrate a pig, Jay! I do not know how to keep a newborn's head from falling off. And I sure as hell don't know how to tell a girl what to do when she gets her period. What the fuck are we going to say? I am familiar with hemostatic dressings, not t-tampons."

I stopped and turned to him before opening the back door. His pale cheeks were cool to the touch as I cupped his face. "Take a breath, sweetheart. In... out. There." I leaned in and pressed a long kiss to his lips before pulling back. "We have a few minutes before we'll need to know how to talk her through her first period. And we have a lot of friends who are very familiar with the care and keeping of lady parts."

Lane's eyes narrowed. "We're not asking your cousin Kandi."

"Oh, fuck no," I agreed happily before towing him out to the truck. "After she brought boxed wine and a crowbar to the baby shower, she's definitely off the list."

"It was a nice crowbar," Lane admitted. "I used it to get the lid off the feed bucket the other day."

I nodded sagely. "She's on the list of our go-to about handy tools, but nothing else."

As we pulled out of the driveway, the fading sound of peacock squawks wished us luck—not just from Dave and his bros but from the four peahens we'd purchased ("because Dave deserves a harem for bringing us together," Lane had insisted) and the several clutches of chicks they'd hatched since then.

Somehow, the sound of the Proud as a Peacock flock brought home the reality of what we were doing.

"We're having a baby today," I said in wonder as we drove past the camellia that Tucker and Dunn had given us as a housewarming gift and the elaborate mailbox stand wrapped in woven wisteria vines.

Lane sighed. "We're having a baby today."

I glanced over at him. "You're going to be an incredible father. You're smart, caring, and kind. I wouldn't want anyone else to be my kids' father, Lane."

He turned to me with suspiciously moist eyes. "Stop it."

I smiled as I turned back to watch the road. The silence sat heavily and expectantly between us.

"Jay?"

"Yeah, baby."

"Thank you for believing in me. And thank you for loving me. You're going to love our daughter so well. I feel just as lucky. I'm just…"

"Scared."

"Terrified."

I pulled up our joined hands and kissed the back of his. "I've heard it's normal. Half that baby shower advice journal was basically people saying we're going to fuck up, and that's all part of it."

He took in a ragged breath and let it out. "Yeah. 'You're fucked, but you're in good company' is not as reassuring as they probably thought it was."

It didn't take us long to get to the hospital, and when we finally got into the maternity ward, Lane seemed shocked by the crowd in SaraCate's room.

"Why have they let all of these people in here? The woman's in labor, for God's sake!"

I squeezed his hand. "Babe, you've met the Winchell family. They're a little…"

Pete sidled up to us. "Unbearable? Overwhelming? *Gauche?*"

"Spirited," I insisted. "And obviously incredibly generous. Your sister especially."

Pete dragged in a long-suffering sigh. "Agreed. But let's not forget this situation is helping her follow her dream."

Lane waved a hand in the air. "Sending her to art school is nothing compared to the gift she's giving us. She's an angel on Earth."

"Get the fuck away from me," a familiar feminine voice snapped. "You're not putting a needle in my spine. I'd rather shove a bowling ball out of my—"

"Sister dear," Pete sang in a loud voice. "Your baby daddies are here."

"Oh, thank God. Lane, tell me you brought pork rinds."

Lane flicked a startled glance at me. I shook my head and stepped ahead of him. "Know what we brought? Our Lamaze breathing techniques and strong hands for massaging—"

"Fuck breathing," she said in a strangled voice, grasping her giant belly with one hand and holding out the other to Lane. "Give me screaming. Give me cussing. Give me a fucking hand to squeeze, damn it!"

Mrs. Winchell, SaraCate and Pete's mother, stood to the side, wringing her own hands. "I really think you should let them do the epidural, honey. Remember last time you wished you'd—"

"I know what I'm doing, Mama," she gritted out, shooting me a pleading look. We'd talked about how she might come to a point of needing family intervention on account of her "daddy's delicate temperament." Sure enough, Tony Winchell sat in a recliner in the corner, staring at his daughter on the bed as if she had aliens for arms and honeysuckle vines growing out of her ears. His eyes never blinked, and his lips appeared to be turning a little blue.

In high school, their daughter had learned accidentally she was pretty good at being pregnant. She'd also learned she was not at all interested in becoming a mother until "the sun set over... wherever the hell the sun never sets."

"Alrighty," I began, plastering on a big fake smile. "It seems like any minute now, Nurse Erin is going to pop her head up and force everyone out, so why don't we all go ahead and say our goodbyes?"

Tony bolted up and dropped a kiss and a "good luck, darlin'" on SaraCate's forehead before making a beeline for Kentucky. Or at least as far as he could get on his own two feet. Mrs. Winchell sighed and approached her daughter. "You're going to do great, honey. Are you sure you don't want me to stay?"

I could see my husband's hand turn white under the hard squeeze from SaraCate's grip. "No, thanks, Mama. The boys are gonna help, and this is their show."

Lane and I knew this was part of the script we'd agreed on earlier, but I still felt guilty. In actuality, she wanted to save her family from bonding with the baby right away and make sure the first time they met her, she was in our arms instead of SaraCate's. We'd given her every opportunity to set her own terms, and she'd decided this was for the best.

It didn't make it any easier.

Once everyone but Pete was gone, he walked over and brushed her hair back from her forehead before meeting her eyes. "You're the strongest woman I know, and fuck you for doing this for them before you could do it for me."

She huffed out a laugh. "You said you never wanted kids. In fact, you said hell would freeze first."

He shrugged. "I don't particularly... but what if I meet the man of my dreams and he does?"

"*Peter?*"

We all spun around at the sound of Dr. Nolan Burch's deep voice as he froze in the doorway to the room.

Pete stared in shock at SaraCate's ob-gyn. Then, without saying a word, he bolted past us, past Dr. Burch, and down the hall.

Lane murmured, "At the rate he's going, he might just catch up to his dad."

"How do you know my brother?" SaraCate asked breathlessly after coming off another contraction.

Dr. Burch frowned, glancing back over his shoulder before proceeding into the room to check his patient. "Peter's your brother?"

SaraCate blew a hair out of her eyes. "Yeah. We have the same name. It's not that common."

"I, ah... I never knew his last name."

Before any of us could ask him why he was being so strange about it, SaraCate screamed with another contraction. The doctor scrambled to check her progress, and within moments, she was pushing.

I quickly moved around the other side of the bed to give SaraCate another hand to break.

"You're doing amazing," Lane said, focusing on her face and encouraging her with a calm voice despite his nerves. "Deep, slow—"

"*Hee-hee-hoooooo.*" She ignored his advice and panted shallowly. The doctor encouraged her to keep doing what she was doing. Meanwhile, I nearly fainted from trying to control everyone's breathing by modeling good behavior.

My head spun, and my face heated. "Babe?" Lane asked, glancing over and catching sight of me.

"It's okay," I whispered, trying to believe it. "Gonna be okay."

"One big push, SaraCate," the doctor urged. "That's it."

Suddenly, SaraCate's giant groan was followed by a long, drawn-out moment of silence that was pierced by a baby's wail.

"She's here," Dr. Burch said with a smile, plopping the messy bundle of newborn on SaraCate's chest. "You did great."

SaraCate's eyes filled with tears as she looked back and forth between us and the baby. Then she gave us a tremulous smile. "She's here. Your daughter's here. I did it. I kept her safe for you."

Warm tears streamed down my face as I watched the world's most incredible miracle take place in real time. Sara-Cate reached out for my hand to put it on the baby's back and then urged Lane to do the same. The three of us held on to her together as she squirmed and blinked.

"What's her name gonna be?" SaraCate asked softly.

"Abigail," Lane and I said together, locking eyes.

I cleared my throat. "It means 'my father's joy.'"

After a while, when SaraCate was somewhat recovered and I was sitting shirtless in the recliner with Abbie on my chest, visitors streamed in. Everyone had brought gifts for SaraCate and generally celebrated her generosity. Lane and I were thrilled to see everyone pamper her the way we'd been doing for months and planned to keep on doing as long as she'd let us.

Lane came over and propped himself on the armrest of the recliner, leaning in to put his arm around me and place his other hand on our daughter's little round bottom. "She's gorgeous."

"She's got a pair of lungs on her. Did you hear earlier?"

"Of course. She sounded like her daddy when the Bovines are down a couple points at the end of the game," Lane said.

I laughed. Bless the man for trying, but he was not a football fan. If he was, he'd know the Bovines hadn't been just a couple of points away from victory in a decade. "And did you see the side-eye she threw at the nurse when they wanted to put the hat with the bow on her? Our baby girl has opinions..."

"Yeah," Lane sighed.

"...like her papa when it comes to the love life of our tenant in the apartment over the garage." I gave my husband a look.

Lane rolled his eyes even as he cuddled closer. "I'll have you know, matchmaking is a time-honored Thicket tradition, Jaybird. And is it such a bad thing to want everyone to find love and happiness like we did?"

"Not at all." I wrapped an arm around his neck and pulled him down to press our lips together. "No regrets, then?" I teased, already knowing what his answer would be since Lane had never given me a single reason to doubt it.

"Regret Entwinin' myself to the best man in the universe? Regret working at a practice where I'm making a real difference? Regret moving to a town I love and that loves me back?" He shook his head. "Not for a single second, I found more in the Thicket than I ever dreamed." He traced Abbie's head with one gentle finger. "My life here is..."

"Perfect?" I teased.

He grinned. "Better than perfect. It's just right." He kissed me again. "And it's ours. Together."

———

Want more Licking Thicket romance? Get ready to head out

Lucy Lennox & May Archer

*on a hilarious, action-packed adventure with the men of
Champion Security, a Licking Thicket spin-off series!*

Hijacked (Carter & Riggs)
Hitched (Quinn & Champ)
Hacked (Kev & Hux)

Letter from Lucy & May

Dear Reader,

Thank you so much for reading *Peacocks*! If this is your first book by one of us and you'd like to read more, we suggest you start with *Fakers*, book one in the Licking Thicket series, or Lucy's *Borrowing Blue* and May's *The Date*.

We would love it if you would take a few minutes to review *Peacocks* on Amazon, Goodreads, or BookBub. Reader reviews really do make a difference and we appreciate every single one of them.

The first book in the Licking Thicket spin-off series, Champion Security, is Carter's story and, needless to say, our favorite "heart doctor" will *not* be content to just settle down and fall in love in the Thicket. His path to love is one heck of an adventure and we can't wait for you to read it. Grab *Hijacked* here → http://readerlinks.com/l/1702712

Our most recent cowritten series is set in another delightful small town and you can go here → https://readerlinks.com/l/3077980 to check out all the shenanigans in Honeybridge, Maine.

Be sure to follow both of us on your favorite retailer site to be notified of new releases, and look for us on Facebook for sneak peeks of upcoming stories. You can also join both of us on Patreon for exclusive content and behind-the-scenes glimpses. Find Lucy here → https://readerlinks.com/l/4255454 and May here → https://readerlinks.com/l/4255455!

Feel free to sign up for our newsletters, stop by www.Lucy-Lennox.com, www.MayArcher.com, or visit Lucy's Lair and Club May on Facebook to stay in touch.

Happy reading!
Lucy & May

More From Lucy and May

Licking Thicket

Flakes

Fakers

Liars

Fools

Turkeys

Peacocks

Champion Security

Hijacked

Hitched

Hacked

Honeybridge

Firecracker

Mr. Important

About Lucy Lennox

Lucy Lennox is the USA Today bestselling author of over fifty gay romance titles including the GoodReads Hall of Fame winner Wilde Love. Born and raised in the southeast USA, she is finally putting good use to that English Lit degree she earned before the turn of the century.

Lucy enjoys naps, pizza, and procrastinating. She stays up way too late each night reading romance because it's simply the best.

For more information and to stay updated about future releases, sales and audio news and to grab some free and bonus reads, please sign up for Lucy's author newsletter on her website at LucyLennox.com or to stay in the know, join her exciting reader group, Lucy's Lair on Facebook.

facebook.com/lucylennoxmm

instagram.com/lucylennoxmm

amazon.com/Lucy-Lennox/e/B01N0IOYPT

bookbub.com/authors/lucy-lennox

patreon.com/lucylennox

pinterest.com/lucy_lennox

Also by Lucy Lennox

Find me online → https://linktr.ee/LucyLennox

Read my books:

Made Marian Series

Forever Wilde Series

Aster Valley Series

The Billionaire Brotherhood Series

After Oscar Series (with Molly Maddox)

Twist of Fate Series (with Sloane Kennedy)

Licking Thicket Series (with May Archer)

Champion Security Series (with May Archer)

Honeybridge Series (with May Archer)

Find a complete list of my stand alone romances and novellas at www.LucyLennox.com along with audio samples, freebies, suggested reading order, and more!

About May Archer

May is an M/M author who lives in Boston. She spends her days planning vacations, mainlining diet soda, avoiding the gym, reading M/M romance, and when all other forms of procrastination fail, writing it.

Visit her website at mayarcher.com to sign up for her newsletter to hear about sales and upcoming releases, freebies and behind the scenes info and more! Or join her Facebook group, Club May!

facebook.com/may.archer.author

instagram.com/mayarcherauthor

amazon.com/May-Archer/e/B075JQVGLX

patreon.com/MayArcherRomance

bookbub.com/authors/may-archer

Also by May Archer

Find me online → https://linktr.ee/mayarcherauthor

Love in O'Leary Series

Whispering Key Series

The Sunday Brothers Series

Copper County Series

The Way Home Series

Licking Thicket Series

(*cowritten with Lucy Lennox*)

Champion Security Series

(*cowritten with Lucy Lennox*)

Honeybridge Series

(*cowritten with Lucy Lennox*)

For a comprehensive list of titles, audio samples, freebies, suggested reading order, and more, visit my website at www.MayArcher.com!

9 781954 857483